Pia's Chest
With

Under other circumstances, Hawk thought, he might have been able to enjoy the show.

"So I'm somehow responsible for your disappearing act?" Pia demanded.

He quirked a brow. "No, but let's agree both of us were putting on an act that night, shall we?"

Heat stained Pia's cheeks. "I turned out to be exactly who I said I was!"

"Hmm," he said, studying her upturned face. "*You* lied to *me*." He well recalled that night three years ago. After he'd accompanied her back to her apartment—a little studio on Manhattan's far Upper East Side—she'd…lured him into unintentionally taking her virginity.

Damn it. Even in his irresponsible younger days, he'd vowed never to be a woman's first lover. He didn't want to be remembered. He didn't want to remember. It didn't mesh with his carefree lifestyle.

Pia stared at him in mute fury and then turned on her heel. "This time, I'm the one walking away. Goodbye, your Grace."

Not for long, he thought.

Dear Reader,

I've always wanted to write a series of books with aristocratic grooms. And Pia and Hawk's romance not only involves an aristocratic groom, but it's also the closest story to a true fairy tale that I've ever written.

Pia is a once-burned-twice-shy romantic wedding planner. And Hawk is the man who keeps her burning up! I hope you sigh some and laugh some while reading their story.

I also hope you enjoy reading more about the secondary characters in this book. Tamara and Sawyer star in *His Black Sheep Bride,* and Belinda and Colin have their story coming soon from Desire!

Warmest wishes,

Anna

ANNA DePALO

ONE NIGHT
WITH PRINCE
CHARMING

Published by Silhouette Books
America's Publisher of Contemporary Romance

For Olivia and Nicholas. Mommy loves you!

SILHOUETTE BOOKS

ISBN-13: 978-0-373-73088-9

Recycling programs for this product may not exist in your area.

ONE NIGHT WITH PRINCE CHARMING

Printed in U.S.A.

ANNA DePALO

A former intellectual property attorney, Anna DePalo lives with her husband, son and daughter in New York City. Her books have consistently hit the Borders bestseller list and Nielsen BookScan's list of top 100 bestselling romances. Her books have won the *RT Book Reviews* Reviewers' Choice Award, the Golden Leaf and the Book Buyer's Best, and have been published in more than a dozen countries. Readers are invited to surf to www.annadepalo.com, where they can join Anna's mailing list.

Dear Reader,

Yes, it's true. We're changing our name! After more than twenty-five years of being part of Harlequin Enterprises, Silhouette Books will officially seal the merger by taking the company's name.

So if you notice a few changes on the covers starting April 2011—Silhouette Special Edition becoming Harlequin Special Edition, Silhouette Desire becoming Harlequin Desire, and Silhouette Romantic Suspense becoming Harlequin Romantic Suspense—don't be concerned.

We'll continue to have the same fantastic authors, wonderful stories, eye-catching covers and emotional, compelling reads. We're just going to be moving under the overall company name, which will make us even easier for you to see in the stores, on the internet and wherever you usually find us!

So look for the new logo, but remember, beneath the image will be the same promise of romantic stories of love, passion, adventure, family and a whole lot more. Just the way you like them!

Sincerely,

The Editors at Harlequin Books

One

She'd just witnessed a train wreck.

Oh, no, not a literal one, Pia shook her head now at the wedding reception. But a figurative one was just as bad.

It was funny what a train wreck looked like from one end of a church aisle, with yards of ivory satin on display and the mingled scents of lilies and roses in the June air. As a wedding planner, she'd dealt with plenty of disasters. Grooms with cold feet. Brides who'd outsized their wedding dress. Even, once, a ringbearer who'd swallowed one of the rings. But surely Pia's always-practical close friend would have no such problems at her wedding. Or so Pia had thought up until about two hours ago.

Of course, the passengers in their pews had all been agape as the Marquess of Easterbridge had stridden purposely up the aisle and announced that, in fact, there *was* an objection to Belinda Wentworth marrying Tod Dillingham. That, in fact, Belinda's hasty and secret marriage to Colin Granville, current Marquess of Easterbridge, had never been annulled.

Collectively, the cream of New York City society had blinked. Eyes had widened and eyebrows had shot up in the pews of St. Bart's, but no one had been so gauche as to actually faint—or pretend to.

And for that, Pia was grateful. There was only so much a wedding planner could do once the dog ate the cake, or the cab splattered mud on the bride's dress, or, as in this case, *the legal husband,* for God's sake, decided to show up at the wedding!

Pia had sat frozen in her position off the center aisle. Angels, she'd thought absently, were in short supply today.

And on the heels of *that* thought had come another. *Oh, Belinda, why, oh, why didn't you ever tell me about your Las Vegas wedding to, of all people, your family's sworn enemy?*

But in her gut, Pia had already known why. It was an act Belinda regretted. Pia's brow puckered, thinking of what Belinda was dealing with right now. Belinda was one of her two closest friends in New York—along with Tamara Kincaid, one of Belinda's bridesmaids.

And then, Pia heaped some of the blame on herself. Why hadn't she spotted and intercepted Colin, like a good little wedding planner? Why hadn't she stayed at the entrance to the church?

People would wonder why she, the bridal consultant, hadn't known enough to keep the Marquess of Easterbridge away, or why she hadn't been able to stop him before a very public debacle ruined her friend's wedding and Pia's own professional reputation.

Pia felt the urge to cry as she thought of the hit that her young business, Pia Lumley Wedding Productions, would take. The Wentworth-Dillingham nuptials—or more accurately now, *almost*-nuptials—were to have been her most high-profile affair to date. She'd only struck out on her own a little over two years ago, after a few years as an assistant in a large event planning company.

Oh, this was horrendous. A nightmare, really. For Belinda *and* herself.

She'd come to New York City from a small town in Pennsylvania five years ago, right after college. This wasn't the way her dream to make it in New York was supposed to end.

As if in confirmation of her worst fears, right after the bride and both her groom *and* her husband had disappeared at the church, presumably to resolve the irresolvable, Pia had been standing in the aisle when a formidable society matron had steamed toward her.

Mrs. Knox had leaned close and said in a stage whisper, "Pia, dear, didn't you see the marquess approaching?"

Pia had smiled tightly. She'd wanted to say she'd had no idea that the marquess had been married to Belinda, and that, in any case, it wouldn't have done any good to intercept His Lordship if, in fact, he'd still been married to Belinda. But loyalty to her friend had kept her silent.

Mrs. Knox's eyes had gleamed. "You might have avoided a public spectacle."

True. But, Pia thought, even if she had known enough to try to stop him, the marquess had been a man on a mission, and one who had at least sixty pounds and more than six inches on her.

So Pia had done what she *could do* after the fact in order to try to save the day. After a quick consultation with assorted Wentworth family members, she'd encouraged everyone to repair to a show-must-go-on reception at The Plaza.

Now, as Pia looked around at the guests and at the waiters passing to and fro with platters of hors d'oeuvres, the low and steady murmur of conversation allowed her to relax her shoulders even as her mind continued to buzz.

She concentrated on her breathing, a relaxation technique

she'd learned long ago in order to help her deal with stressed-out brides and even more stressful wedding days.

Surely, Belinda and Colin would resolve this issue. *Somehow.* A statement could be issued to the press. With any luck something that began with *Due to an unfortunate misunderstanding…*

Yes, that's right. Everything would be okay.

She shifted her focus outward again and, right then, she spotted a tall, sandy-haired man across the room.

Even though he was turned away from her, the hair at the back of her neck prickled as a sense of familiarity and foreboding hit her. When he turned to speak to a man who'd approached him, she saw his face and sucked in a breath.

And that's when her world *really* came to a screeching halt. In her head, engines collided, the sound of crunching metal mixing with the smell of smoke. Or was the smoke coming out of her ears?

Could this day get any worse?

Him. James Fielding…aka Mr. Wrong.

What was James doing here?

It had been three long years since she'd last seen him, when he'd abruptly entered—and then promptly exited—her life, but there was no mistaking those seduce-you, golden Adonis looks.

He was nearly a decade older than her twenty-seven, but he hardly looked it, damn him. The sandy hair was clipped shorter than she remembered, but he was just as broad, just as muscular and just as impressive at over six feet tall.

His expression was studied rather than the fun-loving and carefree one she'd memorized. Still, a woman never forgot her first lover—especially when he'd vanished without explanation.

Unknowingly, Pia started toward him.

She didn't know what she would say, but her feet impelled her forward, as anger sang in her veins.

Her hands clenched at her sides.

As she approached, she noted that James was speaking with a well-known Wall Street hedge fund manager—Oliver Smithson.

"…Your Grace," the older and graying man said.

Pia's stride faltered. *Your Grace?*

Why would James be addressed as *Your Grace?* The reception room held its share of British aristocrats, but even marquesses were addressed as *My Lord*. As far as she knew, *Your Grace* was a form of address reserved for…dukes.

Unless Oliver Smithson was joking?

Unlikely.

The thought flashed through her mind, and then it was too late.

She was upon them, and James spotted her.

Pia noted with satisfaction the flicker of recognition in his hazel eyes.

He looked debonair in a tuxedo that showcased a fit physique. His facial features were even, though his nose wasn't perfectly sloped, and his jaw was square and firm. Eyebrows that were just a shade darker than his hair winged over eyes that had fascinated her in their changeable hue during their one night together.

If she wasn't so fired up, the impact of all that masculine perfection might have knocked the air from her lungs. As it was, she felt a sizzle skate along her nerve endings.

She could be excused for being a fool three years ago, she told herself. James Fielding was sex poured into civilized attire.

Though his rakish air, so undeniable when she'd first met him, had been tamed, both by his clothes and his demeanor, she sensed that it was still there. She was *intimately* acquainted with it.

"Ah, our lovely wedding planner," Oliver Smithson said, seemingly oblivious to the tension in the air, and then laughed heartily. "Couldn't have predicted this turn of events, could we?"

Pia knew the comment was a reference to the drama at the church, but she couldn't help thinking grimly that it applied just as well to the current situation. She would *never* have expected to run into James here.

As if following her line of thought, James raised an eyebrow.

Before either of them could say anything, however, Smithson went on, addressing her, "Have you made the acquaintance of His Grace, the Duke of Hawkshire?"

The Duke of...?

Pia's eyes went wide, and she stared in mute fury. *So he really was a duke?* Was his name even James?

No, wait—she knew the answer to that question. She had, of course, reviewed the guest list for the wedding. She'd had no idea, however, that her Mr. Wrong and James Carsdale, Ninth Duke of Hawkshire, were one and the same.

She felt suddenly light-headed.

James glanced at Oliver Smithson. "Thank you for attempting to affect an introduction, but Ms. Lumley and I have met before," he said before turning back to her. "And please address me as Hawk. Most people do these days."

Yes, they were more acquainted than anyone could guess, Pia thought acerbically. And how dare Hawk stand there so haughty and self-possessed?

Her gaze clashed with that of the man who was an intimate stranger to her. Angling her chin up, she said, "Y-yes, I-I've had the pleasure."

Immediately, her cheeks flamed. She'd meant to make a sophisticated double entendre, but she'd undermined herself by sounding unsure and naive.

Damn her stutter for making an appearance now. It just showed how flustered she was. She'd worked a long time with a therapist to suppress her childhood speech impediment.

Still, Hawk's eyes narrowed. Without a doubt, he'd understood her intended dig, and he didn't like it. But then his expression turned intense and sensual, before changing again to a perplexing flash of tenderness.

Beneath her sleeveless brown sheath, Pia felt a frisson of awareness, her breasts and abdomen tightening. Surely she was mistaken about that fleeting look that appeared almost tender?

Was he feeling sorry for her? Was he looking down at her, the naive virgin whom he'd left after one night? The thought made her spine stiffen.

"Pia."

As her name fell from his chiseled lips—the first time she'd heard it from him in three years—she was swamped by thoughts of a night of blistering sex between her white embroidered sheets.

Damn him. She rallied her resolve.

"What an unexpected…pleasure," Hawk said, his lips quirking, as if he, too, knew how to play at a game of hidden meaning.

Before she could reply, a waiter stopped beside them and presented them with a platter of canapés with baba ghanoush purée.

Staring down at the appetizers, Pia's first thought was that she and Belinda had spent an entire afternoon choosing the hors d'oeuvres for today.

Then, as another thought quickly followed, she decided to go for broke.

"Thank you," she acknowledged the waiter.

Turning back to the duke, she smiled sweetly. "It's a pleasure to savor. Bon appétit."

Without pausing a beat, she plastered his face with a fistful of eggplant.

Then she turned on her heel and stalked toward the hotel kitchen.

Dimly, she recorded the astonished gazes of the hedge fund manager and a few nearby guests before she slapped open the kitchen's swinging doors. If her professional reputation hadn't already been ruined, it was surely going down in flames now. *But it was worth it.*

Hawk accepted the cloth napkin from the waiter who came scurrying over.

"Thank you," he said with appropriate aristocratic sang-froid.

He carefully wiped baba ghanoush from his face.

Oliver Smithson eyed him. "Well…"

Hawk wiped his lips against each other. "Delicious, though a bit on the tart side."

Both the appetizer and the petite bombshell who'd delivered it.

The hedge fund manager laughed uneasily and cast a look around them. "If I'd known the Wentworth wedding would be this exciting, I'd have shorted it."

"Really?" Hawk drawled. "This is one stock that I'm betting won't fall in price. In fact, isn't notoriety the route to fame and fortune these days? Perhaps the bride will have the last laugh yet."

Hawk knew he had to do what he could to dampen today's firestorm. Despite the affront to his person, he thought of the pixie wedding planner who moments ago had stormed away.

He also wondered where his friend Sawyer Langsford, Earl of Melton, had gone, because right now he could use some help in putting out the blazes that were burning. He was sure Melton could be recruited despite being one of Dillingham's groomsmen. Sawyer was a distant relative and acquaintance of the groom's, but he was an even better friend of Easterbridge's.

Hawk realized that Smithson was looking at him curiously,

obviously debating what, if anything, to say at an awkward moment.

"Excuse me, won't you?" he asked, and then without waiting for an answer, stepped in the direction in which Pia had gone.

He supposed he shouldn't be so dismissive of a valuable business contact, but he had a more pressing matter to attend to.

He flattened his hand against the swinging kitchen door and pushed his way inside.

As he strode in, Pia swung around to face him.

She was unintentionally sexy, just like the first—and last—time they had met. A compact but curvy body was bound in a satin dress that hugged everywhere. Her smooth dark blond hair was caught up in a practical, working-glam chignon. And then there was the smooth-as-satin skin, as well as the bow lips and the eyes that still reminded him of clear amber.

Her eyes flashed at him now, just as Hawk was doing a quick recovery from being hit with all that stop-and-go sexy at once.

"C-come to find me?" Pia demanded. "Well, you're three years too late!"

Hawk had to admire her feistiness, much as it came at his expense at the moment. "I came to check on how you're doing. I assure you that if I'd known you'd be here—"

Her eyes widened dangerously. "You would have what? Run in the opposite direction? Never have accepted the wedding invitation?"

"This meeting comes as much of a surprise to me as it does to you."

A little surprisingly, he hadn't caught a glimpse of her until she'd come upon him at the reception. Of course, he'd been among the throng of four hundred invited guests—and one decidedly *uninvited* one—at the church. And then everyone, including him, had been transfixed by the appearance of

Easterbridge. Who the hell would have known the bride had a husband stashed away—who was none other than London's most famous landowning marquess? But that shock had been nothing compared to the surprise of seeing Pia again…and seeing the mingled astonishment and hurt on her face.

"An unfortunate surprise, I'm sure, *Your Grace,*" Pia retorted. "I don't recall you mentioning your title the last time we met."

A direct hit, but he tried to deflect it. "I hadn't succeeded to the dukedom at the time."

"But you weren't simple Mr. James Fielding, either, were you?" she countered.

He couldn't argue with her point there, so he judiciously chose to remain silent.

"I thought so!" she snapped.

Hell. "My full name is James Fielding Carsdale. I am now the Ninth Duke of Hawkshire. I was formerly entitled to be addressed as Lord James Fielding Carsdale or simply—" his lips twisted in a self-deprecating smile "—Your Lordship, though I usually preferred to dispense with the title and the formality that came with it."

The truth was that, back in his playboy days, he had grown used to moving around incognito simply as Mr. James Fielding—thereby avoiding tiresome gold diggers and shaking off the trappings of his position in life—until someone, Pia, had gotten hurt by his charade and his dropping out of sight without a word.

He hadn't even been the heir apparent to his father's ducal title until William, his older brother, had died in a tragic accident, Hawk thought with a twist of the gut. Instead, he'd been Lord James Carsdale, the devil-may-care gadabout younger son who'd dodged the bullet that was the responsibilities of the dukedom—or so he'd thought.

It had taken three years of shouldering those very responsibilities to understand just how thoughtless, how careless, he had been before, and how much damage he might have done. Especially to Pia. But she was wrong if she thought he'd avoid her. He was glad to see her again—glad to have a chance to make amends.

Pia's face drew into a frown. "Are you suggesting that your behavior can somehow be excused because the name you gave me wasn't a total lie?"

Hawk gave an inward sigh. "No, but I am trying, belatedly, to come clean, for what it's worth."

"Well, it's worth nothing," she informed him. "I'd actually forgotten all about you until this opportunity presented itself to confront you about your disappearing act."

They were drawing curious stares from the kitchen staff and even some of the waiters, who were, however, too busy to linger and ogle the latest wedding spectacle.

"Pia, can we take this conversation elsewhere?" Hawk pointedly glanced around them. "We're adding to the events of a day that only needs a little push to tip it over into melodrama."

"Believe me," she retorted, "I've been to enough weddings to know we're nowhere near melodrama. Melodrama is the bride fainting at the altar. Melodrama is the groom flying to the honeymoon by himself. Melodrama is not the bridal consultant confronting her loutish one-night stand!"

Hawk said nothing. He was more concerned for her sake than his, anyway. And she was probably right. What was another scene in a day full of them? Besides, it was clear that Pia was very upset. The wedding disruption had to be troubling her more than she cared to admit, and then there was *his* presence.

Pia folded her arms and tapped her foot. "Do you run out on every woman the morning after?"

No, only on the one and only woman who'd turned out to be a virgin—her. He'd been attracted to her heart-shaped face and compact but shapely body, and the next morning, he'd known he was in too deep.

Hawk wasn't proud of his behavior. But his former self seemed aeons removed from his present situation.

Though even now, he itched to get close to her...to touch her...

He pushed the thought aside. He reminded himself sternly of his course in life ever since he'd become the duke, and that destiny didn't involve messing up Pia's life again. This time, he wanted to make up for what he'd done, for the gift he'd taken from her without realizing...the one she hadn't bothered to warn him about in advance.

Hawk bent toward Pia. "You want to talk about secrets?" he said in a low voice. "When had you been planning to tell me you were a virgin?"

Pia's chest rose and fell with outrage. Under other circumstances, Hawk thought with the back of his mind, he might have been able to enjoy the show.

"So I'm somehow responsible for your vanishing act?" Pia demanded.

He quirked a brow. "No, but let's agree that we were both putting on an act that night, shall we?"

Heat stained Pia's cheeks. "I turned out to be exactly who I said I was!"

"Hmm," he said, studying her upturned face. "As I recall, you disclosed that you'd never had unprotected sex—now who was shading the truth?"

After he'd accompanied her back to her apartment—a little studio on Manhattan's Upper East Side—they'd done the responsible thing before being intimate. He'd wanted to assure her that he was clean and, in return, she'd...lulled him into unintentionally taking her virginity.

Damn it. Even in his irresponsible younger days, he'd vowed never to be a woman's first lover. *He didn't want to be remembered. He didn't want to remember.* It didn't mesh with his carefree lifestyle.

But she'd claimed to have forgotten him. Was it pride alone

that had made her toss out that put down—or was it true? Because he hadn't succeeded in getting her out of his mind, much as he'd tried.

As if in answer to his question, Pia stared at him in mute fury, and then turned on her heel. "Th-this time, I'm the one walking away. Goodbye, Your Grace."

She strode away from him and deeper into the recesses of the kitchen, leaving Hawk to brood alone about their chance encounter—the perfect cap to a perfectly awful day. Pia had been nonplussed, to say the least, by his unexpected appearance and her discovery of who he really was.

But it was also clear that Pia was worried—Belinda's almost-wedding couldn't have good consequences for Pia's wedding planning business. And the fact that Pia herself had given him an unexpected taste of baba ghanoush before some stupefied guests couldn't have helped matters, either.

Pia obviously needed help. For, despite tasting eggplant and their angry confrontation, he still felt an overriding and overdue obligation to make amends.

And with that thought, Hawk contemplated a burgeoning idea.

Two

When Pia got home from the reception at The Plaza, she did *not* conduct an exorcism to banish Hawk from her life again. She did not create a likeness of him with ice cream sticks to ceremonially take apart.

Instead, after picking up and removing Mr. Darcy from her computer chair, she went straight to Google and typed in Hawk's name and title. She told herself it was so she could find a photo to make an Old West sheriff's poster: WANTED: RENEGADE DUKE MASQUERADING AS MR. RIGHT. In reality, she was thirsty for information now that she had Mr. Wrong's real name.

James Fielding Carsdale, Ninth Duke of Hawkshire.

The internet did not disappoint her. It offered up a bounty of hits in a few seconds.

Hawk had started Sunhill Investments, a hedge fund, three years ago, shortly after he'd—she let herself think it—taken her virginity and run. The company had done very well, making Hawk and his partners multimillionaires many times over.

Drat. It was hard to accept that after his dumping of her, he'd been visited with good fortune rather than feeling the wrath of cosmic justice.

Sunhill Investments was based in London, but had recently opened an office in New York—so Hawk's presence on this side of the Atlantic might be for more than the Wentworth-Dillingham wedding that wasn't.

As Pia delved beyond the first few hits, she absently scratched Mr. Darcy's ears as he stroked by her legs. She'd adopted the cat from a shelter close to three years ago and taken him back to the two-bedroom apartment that she'd just moved into—still, however, on the less fashionable edge of Manhattan's Upper East Side.

The fact that the apartment was rent-stabilized and also served as a tax-deductible office permitted her to afford a place that was on the outer fringes of the world that she wanted to tap into—that of Upper East Side prep school girls and future debutantes with well-heeled parents and with living quarters in cloistered prewar buildings guarded by uniformed and capped doormen standing under ubiquitous green awnings.

She'd decorated the apartment as a showcase for her creativity and style because she had the occasional visit from a potential client. Mostly, however, she traveled to see brides in their well-appointed and luxurious homes.

Now, she clicked on her computer mouse. After a few minutes, she brought up a link with an old article about Hawk from the *New York Social Diary.* He was pictured standing between two blond models, a drink in hand and a devilish glint in his eye. The article made it clear that Hawk had been a regular on the social circuit, mostly in London and somewhat in New York.

Pia's lips tightened. Well, at least the article served as some confirmation that she was his physical type—he appeared to have an affinity for blondes. However, at five-foot-four, she was a few inches shorter—not to mention a bit fleshier—than the leggy, skinny catwalkers he'd been photographed with.

The only saving grace in the whole situation was that Hawk's detestable behavior three years ago had given her the courage to embark on her own and start her namesake wedding planning business. She'd realized it was time to stop waiting for Prince Charming and take charge of her life. How pathetic would it have been if he'd been scaling the heights of the financial world while she'd been pining away for him, cocooned to this day in the studio apartment where she'd lived three years ago?

She'd moved on and up, just as he had. And Hawk—the duke or His Grace or however he liked to be referred to— could take a flying leap with his millions.

Still, she couldn't help digging for further information online. It was an exercise in self-flagellation to understand the extent to which she'd been a naive virgin who'd given away the goods to a smooth-talking playboy.

After a half hour of searching, she discovered that Hawk's reputation didn't disappoint. He'd dated models, actresses and even a chanteuse or two. He'd been part of the social whirl of people with money to spare even before his recent incarnation as a top financier.

How unworldly she'd been to expect more than one night with him. How stupidly trusting.

And yet, she reminded herself, it hadn't only been naiveté. She'd been tricked—duped—and used by a practiced player.

She pushed away from the computer screen and padded into her bedroom. Her mind on autopilot, she removed her brown satin dress and slipped into cotton striped pajama bottoms and a peach-colored sleeveless top. In the bathroom, she removed her makeup, moisturized her face and brushed her teeth.

Walking back into the bedroom again, she began to take the pins from her hair as she moved to her dressing table—bought used at a flea market—and sat down. When her hair was loose, she ran a brush through it and stared at herself in the mirror.

She'd never been glamorously beautiful, but she'd been able to lay some claim—if the occasional comments she'd received since high school were to be believed—to being a sort of *cute pretty.* Now, though, she forced herself to be more critical.

Was there something about her that screamed *Take advantage of me?* Did her face sing *I'm a pushover?*

She sighed as she stood, switched off the bedside lamp and slid into bed. She felt Mr. Darcy spring onto the bed and curl his warm weight next to her leg.

Pia turned her face to the window, where rain had begun to pelt the glass, blurring the illumination cast by the city lights outside.

It had been a long, too eventful day, and she was bone-tired. But instead of weariness overtaking her, she found herself awake.

In the privacy of her bedroom, in her own bed and covered by the shadows of the night, she was surprised by the sudden moisture of tears on her face—a reflection of the rain outside. She hadn't cried over Hawk in a long time.

Since she'd switched apartments, Hawk had never invaded this sanctum. But he'd slept in this bed.

Drat Hawk.

With any luck, she'd never have to see him again. She was over him, and this would be the absolute last time that she'd shed tears about him.

Déjà vu. Hawk looked around him at Melton's picturesque Gloucestershire estate, which wasn't so different from his own family seat in Oxford. The centuries-old limestone estate was surrounded by acres of pastoral countryside, which was in full greenery in the August warmth. They could and did set period movies in places like this.

Except his friend Sawyer Langsford, Earl of Melton, was going to have a very real wedding to The Honorable Tamara Kincaid, a woman who could barely be persuaded to dance with him at the Wentworth-Dillingham near-miss of a wedding two months ago.

At the thought of weddings, Hawk admitted to himself that he'd reached a point in his life when his professional life had quieted down a bit, and at age thirty-six, the responsibility to beget an heir for the dukedom had begun to weigh on him.

In his younger, more carefree days, he'd dated a lot of women. In fact, he'd reveled in distinguishing himself as the bon vivant younger son—in spite of his steady job in finance—in contrast to his more responsible older brother, the heir.

And now one of his closest friends was getting married. Hawk had come at Sawyer's request for what was to be a small wedding in the presence of family and close friends. Easterbridge would also be present, and heaven help them, at the bride's invitation, so would his wife, Belinda Wentworth—without, however, her almost-husband, Tod Dillingham.

And Hawk had it on good authority that none other than Pia Lumley would be the wedding planner today. He'd been forewarned by Sawyer. For, as circumstances would have it, Tamara Kincaid was another good friend of Pia's.

As if conjured by his thoughts, Pia walked out from the French doors leading to the stone terrace at the back of the house, and then down to the grassy lawn where Hawk stood.

She looked young, fresh and innocent, and Hawk felt a sudden pang. She'd been all those things three years ago when he'd first met her—and left her.

She was wearing a white shirt with cuffs rolled back beyond her elbows and lime-green cotton pants paired with pink ballet flats. The pants hugged her curves, and just a hint of cleavage was visible at the open collar of her shirt. Her smooth blond hair was caught in a ponytail, and her lips looked shiny and full.

Hawk felt a tightening in his gut.

Despite having been plastered with eggplant at their last meeting, he felt drawn to her. She had sex appeal without being contrived—so different from many of the women in his social circle.

She was everything he wanted, and everything he couldn't have. It would throw him off track from the life that he was supposed to be living now if he got involved with her again. He had put his playboy days behind him.

He was thirty-six, and he'd never been more aware of his responsibilities than since he'd succeeded to the dukedom. Among other things, he had a duty to produce an heir to secure a centuries-old title. And in the normal course of events, he would be expected to marry someone of his class and social station—certainly his mother expected that of him.

In the past year, his mother had taken it upon herself to bring him into contact with eligible women, including, particularly, Michelene Ward-Fombley—a woman whom some had speculated would have made a wonderful duchess for his older brother, before William's untimely death.

He pushed aside thoughts about his most recent transatlantic phone conversation with his mother, and the unspoken expectations that had been alluded to…

Instead, Hawk couldn't help noting now that Pia resembled an enticing wood sprite. She was clearly unafraid to wear flats with her petite frame for a working casual look on a tepidly warm August day typical for this part of England. In his own nod to the weather, he had dispensed with anything but a white shirt and tan pants.

Pia looked up and spotted him as she walked across the lawn.

He watched as she hesitated.

After a moment, she continued to move toward him, but

with obvious reluctance. He was clearly standing in the direct path of her intended destination—very likely, the pavilion on the property that would serve as one of the backdrops for the wedding.

He tried to break the ice. "I know what you're thinking."

She gave him a haughty, disbelieving look.

"We don't see each other for three years," he pressed on, "and now we somehow run into each other for the second time in two months."

"Believe me, it's no more pleasant for me than it is for you," she responded, coming to a stop before him.

He scanned her face, angling his head to the side.

He pretended to make his perusal casual, joking even. Still, he caught the way a stray strand of sun-kissed honey-blond hair caressed her cheek gently. He stopped himself from reaching out to touch her soft skin and run his thumb over the outline of her jaw.

Then he made the mistake of picking up the light scent of lavender that he'd associated with her ever since their first night together. He couldn't help being attracted to her—he just couldn't act on that attraction.

"Wh-what are you doing?" she demanded.

"I'm checking to see if you're hiding hors d'oeuvres or canapés somewhere. I wanted to be prepared for another missile attack."

His attempt at a jest was met with a frosty look.

Pia raised her chin. "I'm here to make sure this wedding proceeds without a hitch."

"Ah, trying to rehabilitate your image?"

He'd meant to tease and test, and at her momentarily arrested look, he realized he'd guessed correctly.

Pia was still worried about her business. Belinda Wentworth's almost-wedding had likely blemished Pia's professional reputation.

In a moment, however, Pia recovered herself, and her

eyes sparked. "My only concern is that you and your two compatriots, Easterbridge and Melton, are in attendance. I have no idea why another friend of mine would get mixed up with a friend of yours. Look at what Easterbridge did to Belinda!"

"What Colin did to Belinda?" Hawk asked rhetorically. "You mean speaking up as *her husband?*"

Pia narrowed her eyes and pressed her lips together.

Hawk had started out this conversation trying to put Pia at ease, but ruffling her feathers was proving to be irresistible. "I defer to your superior experience with wedding etiquette. Are husbands even allowed to speak?"

"The marquess needn't have done so at the wedding. A nice, private communication from his attorney to hers would have sufficed."

"Perhaps Easterbridge had little notice of Belinda's impending wedding to Dillingham. Perhaps he did what he could to prevent a crime from occurring." Hawk arched a brow. "Bigamy is a crime in many places, including New York, you know."

"I'm well aware of that!"

"I'm relieved to hear it."

Pia gave him a repressive look, and then eyed him suspiciously. "How much notice did you have of Easterbridge's actions?"

"I wasn't even aware that Easterbridge was married to Belinda."

Hawk was glad he could set the record straight because Pia obviously suspected him of double-dealing as a wedding guest of Dillingham's but a friend of Easterbridge's. Not only hadn't he known about Easterbridge's past marriage, but he suspected that the only reason he'd been invited to the wedding in June was because Dillingham wanted to cement important social ties, however tenuous up to that point.

"And *I* have no idea what would have made Belinda wed

a friend of yours two years ago, in Las Vegas, of all places," Pia countered.

"Perhaps my friends and I are irresistible," he replied mockingly.

"Oh, I'm well aware that you're irresistible to women."

Hawk raised his brows and wondered whether Pia was admitting to her own past susceptibility to him. Had *she* found him not merely attractive but irresistible? Had she fallen into bed with him because she'd been swept up in the moment and carried away by passion?

"Once I had your real name, a little internet search revealed a good deal of information," Pia elaborated, dashing his hopes that she'd been referring to herself when she'd called him irresistible.

Hawk had no doubt as to what an internet search had revealed. He mentally winced at the thought of the news reports and gossip that must have come up about his younger, more spirited days. The women…the carousing…

"You know, I suppose I should have been wary three years ago when my Google search on James Fielding turned up nothing in particular, but then I supposed *Fielding* was such a common name…"

He quirked his lips. "My ancestors are no doubt rolling in their graves at being labeled *common*."

"Oh, yes, pardon me, *Your Grace*," Pia returned bitingly. "You can rest assured that I'm no longer ignorant of the protocol due to your rank."

Damn protocol to hell, he wanted to respond. It was one of the reasons he'd preferred flying under the radar as plain James Fielding. Except these days, of course, having succeeded to the ducal title, he could no longer afford such a luxury. Then, too, he was all too cognizant of his responsibilities.

The irony wasn't lost on him that having succeeded to the title of Duke of Hawkshire, he'd gained all manner of wealth—and responsibilities—that most men coveted, but had lost the things he craved most: anonymity, a certain freedom and being valued for himself.

"Tell me about your wedding business," he said abruptly, turning the conversation back in the direction he wanted. "Three years ago, I recall you were still working at a large event planning firm and had big dreams of setting out on your own."

Pia looked guarded and then defiant. "I did manage to start my own business, as you can tell. It was shortly after your abrupt disappearance, in fact."

"Are you saying you have me to thank?" Hawk asked with exaggerated aristocratic hauteur and faint mockery.

Pia's hand curled at her side. "*Thanks,* I think, would be going too far. But I believe it was your abrupt exit that provided me with the impetus to strike out on my own. After all, there's nothing like a momentary disappointment to fuel the drive to succeed in another area of life."

Hawk gave a weak imitation of a smile. He very much regretted his actions in the past, but he wondered what she'd say if she knew the extent of his responsibilities, ducal and otherwise, these days.

"You were very creative with the décor at Belinda's wedding," he said, ignoring her jab in an effort to be more conciliatory. "The gold and lime-green color scheme was certainly unusual."

At Pia's look of momentary surprise, he added, "You needn't look so taken aback that I noticed the detail. After savoring baba ghanoush, I believe contemplating the scenery became a much more engaging pastime."

He had let himself study the décor because he had been curious about any detail that would reveal anything about *her*—and it had beat deflecting curious looks and probing questions from the other wedding guests.

"I'm glad my excellent aim had at least one beneficial consequence," Pia responded dryly.

"Ah, I assume the consequences to your wedding business weren't so satisfactory?" he probed, taking advantage of his opening.

Pia's expression turned defensive, but not before Hawk saw the fleeting distress there.

"What sort of wedding would you have for yourself, Pia?" Hawk asked, his voice suddenly low and inviting. "Surely you must have envisioned it many times."

He knew he was playing with fire, but he didn't care.

"I'm in the wedding business," Pia responded frostily. "Not the romance business."

Their eyes held for moments…until a voice called out Pia's name.

He and Pia turned at the same time to look back in the direction of the house, where Tamara was descending the terrace steps.

"Pia," Tamara announced, coming toward them across the lawn. "I've been looking for you everywhere."

"I was just walking over to the pavilion," Pia responded. "I wanted to see what can be done with it."

Hawk watched as Tamara glanced curiously from Pia to him and back.

"Well, I'm glad I found you," Tamara said, and then hooked her arm through Pia's.

Tamara spared Hawk a cursory look. "You don't mind if I commandeer Pia, do you, Hawk…I mean, Your Grace?" And then not waiting for an answer, she turned Pia toward the pavilion. "I thought not."

Hawk's lips quirked. Tamara wasn't one to stand on ceremony. Though she was the daughter of a British viscount, she'd been raised mostly in the United States and had the decidedly democratic tendencies of the bohemian jewelry designer she was.

She'd also obviously sailed in like a mother hen to rescue Pia.

"Not at all," Hawk murmured to Tamara's retreating back.

He watched the two women cross the lawn.

When Pia turned back briefly to glance at him, he returned her gaze solemnly.

He'd gleaned a lot from their conversation. He'd guessed correctly—as evidenced by her momentary distress just now—that Pia's wedding business needed help in the wake of Belinda's wedding. The fact that Pia's firm had managed to survive for more than two years said something, however.

Pia obviously had talent, and she'd nurtured it since their one night together.

With that thought, as he turned back to the house, Hawk realized that a conversation with his sister, a prospective bride, was in order.

Three

As she and Tamara walked toward the pavilion, Pia noticed her friend glance at her.

"I hope I wasn't interrupting anything," Tamara remarked, and then paused at Pia's continued silence. "On second thought, perhaps I hope I did."

As Tamara suddenly stopped to speak with one of the staff who hailed her, Pia stood nearby and soon found herself lost in thought about the night that she and Hawk had first met.

The beat of the music could be felt in the bar stools, on the tables and along the walls. In fact, everything vibrated. It was loud and packed, bodies brushing past each other in the confines of the tavern.

A bar wasn't her preferred scene, Pia thought, but she'd come here with a coworker from the event-planning business she worked for in order to rub shoulders with bright young things and their beaus.

People who liked a party—and needed event organizers—

usually attended parties prodigiously. And it had almost been a job directive from her boss to be social after work hours, making connections and trying to bring in business.

Except Pia's interest wasn't in anniversary parties or coming-of-age celebrations.

Instead, she liked weddings.

Someday, she promised herself, her dream of having her own wedding planning business would become a reality.

In the meantime, she shouldered her way past other patrons and reached the bar. But at her height, she could barely see above those sitting at the bar stools, let alone signal the bartender.

A man next to her gestured to the bartender and called out an order for a martini.

She glanced up at him and, a second later, sucked in a breath as he looked down at her with an easygoing grin.

"Drink?" he offered.

He was one of the most attractive men she'd ever seen. He was tall, certainly over six feet, his sandy hair slightly tousled, and his hazel eyes, flecked with interesting bits of gold and green, dancing. His nose was less than perfect—had it been broken once?—but that added to his magnetism. His grin revealed a dimple to the right of his mouth.

Most importantly, he was looking at *her* with warm, lazy interest.

He was the closest thing to her fantasy man as she'd ever seen—not that she'd ever admit to anyone that, at twenty-four, she'd had a fantasy lover and no other kind.

Pia parted her lips—*please, please let me sound sophisticated.* "Cosmopolitan, thank you."

He gave the briefest nod of acknowledgment, and then looked away to signal the bartender and order her drink. Within seconds, he effortlessly accomplished what to her had been blocked by multiple obstacles.

When he looked back at her, he was smiling again.

"Are you?" he asked, his low and smooth voice inviting intimacy.

She stalled. "Am I…?"

His eyes crinkled. "Are you a Cosmo girl?"

She pretended to consider the question for a moment. "It depends. Are you a pickup artist?"

He laughed, his expression saying he was respectful of her parry even as his interest sharpened. "I don't suppose you'd give a hint as to what the right answer is supposed to be?"

Pia played along. "Do you need a hint? Doesn't charm get you the answer you want?"

His accent wasn't easy to pinpoint—he appeared to be from here, there and anywhere—but she thought she detected a faint British enunciation.

"Hmm, it depends," he mused, rubbing his chin and showing his dimple again. "Are you here with anyone?"

She knew he meant a man—a date. "I'm here with a coworker, but I seem to have lost track of Cornelia in the crowd."

He looked momentarily intent and seductive beneath his easygoing veneer, but then his casual appeal took over again. "Great, then I can be as charming as I'm able. Let's start with names. No woman as lovely and enchanting as you can be called anything but—?"

He quirked a brow.

She couldn't help smiling. "Pia Lumley."

"Pia," he repeated.

The sound of her name falling from his chiseled lips sent shivers chasing over her skin. He'd called her *lovely* and *enchanting*. Her fantasy man had a voice, and it was dreamy.

"James Fielding," he volunteered.

Just then, the bartender leaned in their direction and slid two drinks across the bar between seated patrons.

James handed the cosmopolitan to her, and then picked up his martini.

"Cheers," he said, clinking his glass against hers.

She took a small sip of her drink. It was stronger than her usual party libation—a light beer or a fruity beach drink was more her style—but then again, she'd wanted to appear sophisticated.

She suspected that James was used to chic women. And she'd grown used to projecting a polished and stylish image when trying to drum up business for work. Potential clients expected it—people didn't want an inexperienced girl from small-town Pennsylvania running their six-figure party.

After sipping from his drink, James nodded at a couple departing from a corner table near them. "Would you like to sit?"

"Thank you," she said, and then turned and slid into a padded booth seat.

As she watched James sit down to her left, a little thrill went through her. So he meant to continue their conversation and further their acquaintance? She was happy she'd held his interest.

She hadn't had many men hit on her. She didn't think she was bad-looking, but she was short and more understated than bold, and therefore easily overlooked. She was cute, rather than one to inspire lust or overwhelming passion.

He looked at her with a smile hovering at his lips. "Are you new to New York?"

"It depends on what you mean by new," she replied. "I've been here a couple of years."

"And you were transported here from a fairy tale called—?"

She laughed. "Cinderella, of course. I'm a blonde."

His smile widened. "Of course."

He rested an arm along the back of the booth seat and reached out to finger a tendril of her hair.

She drew in a breath—hard.

"And a beautiful shade of blond, it is," he murmured. "It's gold spun with wheat and sunshine."

She looked into his eyes. She could, she thought, spend hours studying the fascinating mix of hues there.

James cocked his head, his eyes crinkling. "Okay, Pia," he continued in his smooth, deep voice, "Broadway, Wall Street, fashion, advertising or *The Devil Wears Prada?*"

"None of the above?"

His eyebrows rose. "I've never struck out before."

"Never?" she asked with feigned astonishment. "I'm sorry I ruined your track record."

"Never mind. I trust your discretion will spare my reputation."

They were flirting—or rather *he* was flirting with *her*—and she was, amazingly, holding her own.

It was all exhilarating. She'd never had a man flirt with her this way, and certainly no one of James's caliber.

In fact, though, she wasn't an actress, a banker, a model, or in advertising or publishing. "I'm an event planner," she said. "I organize parties."

"Ah." His eyes gleamed. "A party girl. Splendid."

There were party girls and then there were *party girls,* she wanted to say, but she didn't correct him.

"What about you?" she asked instead. "What are you doing here in New York?"

He straightened, dropping his arm from the back of the seat. "I'm just an ordinary Joe with a boring finance job, I'm afraid."

"There's nothing ordinary about you," she blurted, and then clamped her mouth shut.

He smiled again, his dimple appearing. "I'm flattered you think so."

She lifted her drink for another sip because he and his

smile—and, yes, that dimple—were doing funny things to her insides.

He was studying her, and she tried to remain casual, though he sat mere inches away.

She was very aware of his muscular thigh encased in beige pants on the seat beside her. He wore no tie, and the strong, corded lines of his neck stood in relief against the open collar of his light blue shirt.

He nodded, his eyes fixed at a spot near her collarbone. "That's an interesting necklace you're wearing."

She glanced down, though she knew what he'd be seeing. She wore a sterling silver necklace with a flying fish pendant. In deference to the July heat, she'd worn a sleeveless turquoise blue sheath dress. The pendant was one of her usual accessories.

She'd come directly to the bar from work, and she figured he'd done the same from the way he was dressed. Though he wasn't wearing a suit, his attire qualified as business casual. Work dress code was more relaxed in the summer in the city, especially on a dress-down Friday.

She flushed now, however, at the thought that between the color of her dress and the symbol on her pendant, she resembled nothing so much as a pond with a solitary fish swimming in it.

Drat. Why hadn't she thought of that when she'd dressed this morning?

But James's face held no hint of amusement at her expense—just simple curiosity.

She fingered her pendant. "The necklace was a gift from my friend Tamara, who is a wonderful jewelry designer here in the city. I like to fish."

"A woman after my own heart then."

Pia checked her surprise. Of course, he would be interested in fishing. He was her fantasy man—how could he not be?

"Do you fish?" she asked unnecessarily.

"Since I was three or four," he said solemnly. "What kind of fishing do you do?"

She laughed with a tinge of self-consciousness. "Oh, anything. Bass, trout… There are plenty of lakes where I grew up in western Pennsylvania. My father and grandfather taught me how to bait and cast a line—as well as ride a horse and, uh, m-milk a cow."

She couldn't believe she'd admitted to milking cows. How would he ever think of her as an urban sophisticate now? She ought to have quit while she was ahead.

James looked nothing but fascinated, however. "Horseback riding—even better. I've been riding since I could walk." His eyes glinted. "I can't say the same about milking cows, on the other hand."

She flushed.

"But I sheered a few sheep during a stay at an Australian sheep station."

Pia felt her lips twitch. "Well, then, you've bested me. I concede."

"Good of you," he deadpanned. "I knew sheep would win out."

"I've done some fly-fishing," she asserted.

He smiled. "Point to you. There are not many women who are willing to stand around in muck all day, wearing waders and waiting to get a bite." His smile broadened into a grin. "As petite as you are, I imagine you couldn't wade in very far."

She struck a look of mock offense. "I'll have you know I stood as still as a chameleon on a branch."

"Then I'd have been tempted to drop a frog down the back of your waders," he teased.

"Oh, you would! Don't tell me you have sisters whom you tormented."

"No such luck," he mourned. "I have one sister, but she's

several years younger than I am, and my mother wouldn't have looked well on any pranks."

"I wouldn't have expected she would," she said with mock indignation. "And if you'd attempted to foist a frog on me, I'd have—"

"Yes?"

He was enjoying this.

"I'd have thrown you for a loop!"

"Don't fairy-tale heroines need to get to know a few frogs?" he asked innocently.

"I believe the expression is *kiss a few frogs,*" she replied. "And, no, the requirements have been updated for the twenty-first century. And anyway, I'd know when I kissed a frog."

"Mmm...do you want to put it to the test?"

"I—I—"

What a time for her stammer to make another appearance.

Not waiting for a clearer sign of encouragement, he leaned in, and as her eyelids lowered, gently pressed his lips to her. She felt the momentary zing of electricity, and her lips parted on an indrawn breath. And then his mouth moved over hers, tasting and sampling, giving and receiving.

His lips were soft, and she tasted the faint lingering flavor of his drink as they kissed. The crowd around them receded as she focused on every warm stroke of his mouth against hers.

Just as their kiss threatened to become more heated, he drew back, his expression thoughtful and bemused. "There, how was that?"

She searched his eyes. "Y-you are in no way related to Kermit the Frog."

He grinned. "How about my fishing? Am I reeling you in?"

"A-am I on the hook or are you?"

"James."

The moment was interrupted as he was hailed by someone and turned in the direction of a man coming toward them.

Pia straightened and sat back in her seat, belatedly realizing with some embarrassment that she was still leaning forward.

"The CEO of MetaSky Investments is here, James," the man announced, sparing her a cursory look. "I'll introduce you."

Pia judged the man to be a contemporary of James's. Perhaps he was a friend or a business colleague.

At the same time, she sensed James hesitate beside her. She could tell that whoever this CEO was, it would be valuable for James to meet him. After all, he was important enough for a friend to have sought James out in the crowded bar.

James turned toward her. "Will you—"

"There you are, Pia! I've been searching for you."

Cornelia materialized out of the crowd.

Pia pasted a bright smile on her face as she glanced at James. "As you can see, you no longer need to worry about leaving me alone."

James nodded. "Will you excuse me?"

"Of course."

Pia tamed her disappointment as James rose to depart. She noticed that he didn't say he'd be back. And she knew better than to expect that he would return. She understood—sort of— that these flirtations in bars were fleeting and transient.

On the other hand, the romantic in her believed in kismet. He was the most magnificent man she'd ever met.

And if that had been the last she'd seen of him, she probably would have remembered him as nothing more than a handsome, charming fantasy—a brief glimpse of a fairy-tale prince to brighten her disappointing night. Certainly, the evening began to show few signs of success once they went their separate ways.

Two hours afterward, however, it was hard to keep

disappointment at bay. She hadn't glimpsed James since he'd departed, nor had she had any luck in making potential contacts, aside from handing her business card out to a couple of women who'd expressed a casual interest in retaining an event planner.

Pia sighed as she slid off a bar stool, having settled her tab. Cornelia had departed twenty minutes ago while Pia had still been conversing with a potential client. The woman who'd just vacated the bar stool next to Pia was an office manager at a small real estate firm, and though she'd had someone whom she used to help plan the firm's annual holiday party, she'd been willing to listen to Pia's pitch.

Business development was the part of her job that Pia found most challenging. Coming from Pennsylvania, she didn't have an extensive social network in the city. And it was so disheartening to get the brush-off from strangers. She supposed that telemarketing could be worse, but then again, at least telemarketers only had to deal with rejection by phone rather than face-to-face.

There was no doubt about the high point of the evening. James had shown real interest in *her*—however briefly.

Pia felt her heart squeeze. *Definitely time to leave.*

She'd head home to a rent-stabilized apartment on the unfashionable edge of the Upper East Side. She decided she'd pop in a DVD and lose herself in one of her favorite Jane Austen flicks, spending the rest of the evening forgetting what would never be.

It was a decent feel-good plan. Except as soon as she stepped out of the bar, she realized that it was pouring rain.

Oh, great.

She huddled under the bar's awning and looked down at herself. Even with the platform heels on her beige sandals, she knew her feet—and likely more—were going to get soaked. She'd tucked a small umbrella into her handbag this morning, just in case, but she'd been betting it wouldn't rain when she'd chosen what to wear. The weather report had said showers weren't in the forecast until the wee hours of the morning.

Her one hope was hailing a cab, but she knew one would be scarce in this kind of weather, and in any case, on her salary, taxis were a luxury she tried to avoid. The only alternative was walking to the subway and then making the long hike from the train station to her apartment.

As she stood there, hugging herself for warmth and debating her options, the tavern door behind her opened.

"Need a ride?"

She turned and glanced up. *James.*

Paradoxically, she felt embarrassed—as if she were the one running out on *him,* when in reality he hadn't sought her out again.

"I thought you'd already left," she blurted.

A slow smile spread across his face. "I did, but I came back in. I was conversing with the CEO of MetaSky outside, where we could hear each other and speak with more privacy." He looked around them. "It wasn't raining then."

She blinked. "Oh."

"Do you need a ride?" he asked again, glancing down at her.

She tried for some belated dignity, even as a gust of wind pelted her with raindrops. "I'm f-fine. I'm just debating whether to walk, row or swim home."

His smile spread. "What about a car instead?"

She raised her eyebrows. "How are we ever going to catch an empty cab in this weather?"

She knew that rain made New York City taxis disappear.

"Leave it to me."

She watched as James scanned the street. Two cabs passed them but their lit signs indicated that they were occupied. As the two of them waited, they made idle chitchat.

Close to fifteen minutes later, by a stroke of luck, James spotted a cab letting out a passenger beyond the nearest intersection. He moved swiftly from the shelter of the awning and into the street when the empty cab started to make its way down their block. He raised his arm, a commanding presence, and hailed the cab.

As the rain continued to assault him, he opened the taxi's door and motioned for her to step in.

"What's your address?" he called as she hurried toward him. "I'll tell the driver."

She called it out to him, realizing that he had an excuse to find out where she lived. He made everything appear smooth, charming and effortless.

"Are you leaving? Do you want to share a cab?" she asked as she reached him. "You're getting drenched! I should have offered you the umbrella in my bag but you stepped out so suddenly."

She couldn't stop the flow of words, though she knew she was nearly babbling. She had no idea what direction was home for him, but it seemed churlish not to offer to share the cab that he'd hailed for her. Yet again, he'd handily managed to accomplish something she herself often found difficult, being petite and certainly less imposing.

James looked at her and his lips quirked. Even with his hair getting matted by the rain and his face wet, he looked unbelievably handsome.

"Thanks for the offer," he said.

She wasn't sure if he meant to accept her offer, but once she entered the confines of the cab, she slid across the seat so he would have room to join her.

A moment later, he slid in beside her, folding his tall frame onto the bench seat and answering her unvoiced question.

She felt relief and a happy flutter, even as she also experienced a sense of nervous awareness. She had never left a bar with a man before—she was cautious. But then again, no man had attempted to pick her up in a bar before.

"I live on First Avenue in the high Eighties," she cautioned

James belatedly as he closed the car door. "I don't want to put you out. I don't know in what direction you need to head."

"It's no problem," he said easily. "I'll see you home first."

She noticed that he didn't divulge whether she was taking him out of his way or not.

He leaned forward to the partition separating the front from the backseat and told the cab driver her address. And in no time at all, they were speeding through Manhattan's wet and half-empty streets.

They were content to make some more desultory chitchat as the car ate up the distance to her apartment. She discovered that he was thirty-three to her twenty-four—not ancient by any means, but older and more worldly than the boys she'd dated back in high school and college in Pennsylvania.

Perhaps in order to make the gulf between them seem less so, she shared her dream of opening her own wedding planning business. Surely, he wouldn't think of her as so young and inexperienced if he knew she had plans to be a business owner.

He showed enthusiasm for her plans and encouraged her to proceed with them.

All the while, as thoughts raced through her mind, she wondered if he felt the sexual tension, too. Would she ever see him again?

In no time at all, however, they arrived outside her building.

James turned toward her, searching her eyes in the silence drawing out between them. "Here we are."

"W-would you like to come up?" she asked, surprising herself.

It was a daring move. But she felt as if their evening had been cut short when he'd had to meet with the CEO of MetaSky.

He paused and looked at her meaningfully for a moment. "Sure…I'd love to."

He settled the cab fare, and then they raced up the front stoop of her building, sharing her small umbrella.

She managed to fish out her keys in record time and let them inside. They stumbled into the vestibule and out of the cold and wet.

She lived in a studio on the top floor of a four-story brownstone. At least, however, the rental was hers alone. On a night like tonight, she didn't have to worry about the awkwardly timed arrival of a roommate or two. She'd made the best of her situation by putting up a partition wall to create a separate bedroom, though she couldn't do anything to alter the fact that her windows were the small ones beneath the roof.

As she heard and felt the tread of James's feet behind her on the stairs, she couldn't help feeling nervous about having him step into her little world.

Fortunately, she didn't have much time to dwell on the matter. Within a few minutes, they reached the uppermost floor, and she inserted her key in her door and let them inside.

She dropped her handbag on a chair and turned around in time to see him scanning her apartment.

He dominated the small space even more than she'd anticipated. Here there were no fellow bar patrons to defuse the full force of the magnetism that he exuded. There was no crowd to mitigate the sexual attraction between them.

James's eyes came back to hers. "It's cute."

She'd tried to make the apartment cheerful, as much to lift her own mood as anything else. A tiny table flanked by two chairs and sporting a vase of pink peonies and tulips sat near the door. The kitchen lined one wall, and a love seat guarded the space on the opposite side. Facing the entry, a small entertainment center stood in front of the partition that separated her bedroom from the rest of the space.

Pia knew what lay beyond the partition that shielded what remained of her apartment from James's gaze. A white croquet coverlet covered the full-size bed that occupied most of her sleeping area.

Nervously, she wet her lips. She couldn't keep her eyes from straying to the rain-soaked spots of his shirt. Some of those wet areas clung to the muscles of his arms and shoulders.

She'd never done this before.

"Pia."

Pia found herself jerked from her memories as Tamara closed the space on the lawn between them. Over Tamara's shoulder, she noticed the member of the household staff with whom Tamara had been speaking was heading back toward the stone terrace and French doors at the back of the house.

Hawk was nowhere to be seen. He, too, must have gone indoors.

"I'm sorry to have left you stranded here."

Pia pasted a bright smile on her face. "Not at all. It's all part of the prerogatives of the bride."

And one of her prerogatives, Pia thought, was to stay away from Hawk for the rest of this wedding...

Four

Pia walked along East 79th Street on Manhattan's Upper East Side looking for the correct house number. She'd received a call from Lucy Montgomery yesterday about being hired as a bridal consultant. She hadn't paid much attention to the particulars, but had jumped at the chance for new business because it had been a slow summer.

She hadn't liked to dwell on how much her silent phone was due to the Wentworth-Dillingham wedding being, well, both *more* and *less* than expected. She hadn't been directly to blame for the first part of the debacle. But the hard truth was that if the wedding had been a resounding success, her phone might have been ringing with more interested brides.

True, she'd been called on to help with Tamara's wedding last month. But that had been a small wedding—mainly family—and had transpired in England, so her involvement hadn't counted for much in the eyes of New York society. And while she'd also worked on a wedding in Atlanta over the summer, she'd been retained for that function *before* Belinda's nuptial debacle.

Now, though, on a breezy day in late September, with clouds overhead and the threat of rain in the air, she walked along one of Manhattan's tonier side streets, glad she'd worn her belted trench to ward off the threatening elements and even happier for the possibility of a new client.

Finding the house number she was looking for, she stopped and surveyed the impressive double-width, four-story limestone town house. A tall, black, wrought-iron fence guarded the façade, and flower boxes and black shutters framed tall, plate-glass windows. In the center of the building, stone steps ascended to the double-door front entrance at the parlor level. But instead of windows, the parlor floor boasted French doors embraced by tiny balconies.

There was no doubt that Lucy Montgomery came from money. This house was a well-preserved example of Manhattan's Gilded Age.

Pia ascended the steps and knocked before ringing the doorbell.

Within moments, an older gentleman, dressed in somber black and white rather than a clear uniform, responded. After Pia introduced herself, the butler took her coat and directed her to the parlor.

Pia soon discovered that the parlor was a spectacular room with a high, molded ceiling and a marble mantel. It was decorated in gold and rose and outfitted with antique furniture upholstered in stripes and prints.

She knew she should recognize the furniture style, but for the life of her, she could never remember how to separate Louis XIV style from its successors, Louis XV and Louis XVI. In any case, expensive was expensive.

She sat on one of the couches flanking the fireplace and contemplated her surroundings, taking several deep breaths to calm her nerves. *She'd never needed an account more.*

She hoped she would sufficiently impress Lucy Montgomery. She'd dressed with care, donning a chic and timeless short-sleeved peach dress and beige pumps, and keeping her jewelry to a minimum. She'd chosen wedding colors, even on an overcast day, because they were cheery and they resonated with brides.

At that moment, the parlor door opened, and with surprising promptness, Lucy appeared, a smile on her face.

Her hostess was a slim, attractive blonde of medium height with hazel eyes. She looked crisp in a salmon-colored shirt and knee-length tan skirt cinched by a wide black belt. Her legs stretched down to strappy sandals and showed off a tan that was courtesy, no doubt, of time spent at one of the sand-dusted retreats favored by the rich or famous or both.

Pia guessed that Lucy was around her own age or younger.

She rose from her seat in time to shake her hostess's outstretched hand.

"Thank you for scheduling this appointment on such short notice," Lucy exclaimed, her inflection British. "I was just about to come down the stairs when Ned told me you were here."

"It was no inconvenience, Ms. Montgomery," Pia responded with a smile of her own. "Client service is what my business is all about."

"It's Lucy, please."

"Pia, then."

"Good," Lucy responded happily, and then glanced at the clock. "I'll have tea brought in, if that meets with your approval." She smiled. "We British consider late afternoon to be teatime, I'm afraid."

"Yes, please. Tea would be wonderful."

After Lucy had gone to the door and spoken in low tones with a member of the household staff, she returned to sit on the sofa with Pia.

"Now then," she said. "I'm rather in desperate need of help, I'm afraid."

Pia tilted her head and smiled. "Many brides come to that conclusion at some point during their engagements. May I offer my congratulations, by the way?"

Lucy lit up. "Thank you, yes. My fiancé is American. I met him while working on an off-Broadway play."

Pia's eyebrows rose. "You're an actress?"

"Shakespearean trained, yes," Lucy replied without a hint of boast, and then leaned forward conspiratorially and winked. "He was one of the producers."

Money married money, Pia thought, if only because the people involved tended to move in the same social circles. She'd seen it many times before. And yet, it was clear from the way Lucy lit up that she was in love with her fiancé.

"You see," Lucy explained, "Derek and I were planning to marry next summer, but I've just landed a new role and we need to move up the wedding. Suddenly, everything seems upon us at once. Since I'm currently working in another production—" Lucy spread out her hands helplessly "—I have no time to organize things myself."

"How quickly would you like to wed?"

Lucy gave her an apologetic smile. "I'm hoping for a New Year's Eve wedding."

Pia kept her expression steady. "Three months. Perfect."

"I should say that the church has been booked and that, quite astonishingly, the Puck Building is available for a reception."

Pia's shoulders relaxed. The most important details had been taken care of. Since the church and the reception hall were set for the new date, she wouldn't have to scout locations.

She and Lucy discussed some other details for a few minutes, until Lucy glanced at the door.

"Ah, tea. Perfect," Lucy said as a middle-aged woman,

obviously one of the household help, appeared with a tray of tea.

Pia felt she was going to like Lucy. Her hostess had a sunny disposition, and there was already a lot to suggest that she would be easy to work with.

Lucy leaned forward as the tray was set down on a table in front of them. "Thank you, Celia."

"How do you take your tea?" Lucy inquired as Celia departed, and then shot Pia a teasing, self-deprecating look. "No matter how long I've been in New York, this is teatime for me. You can imagine the problems it causes when I'm giving a matinee performance!"

Before Pia could respond, Lucy glanced toward the door again. "Hawk," Lucy acknowledged with a smile. "How nice of you to join us."

Pia followed the direction that Lucy was looking, and froze.

Hawk. Him.

It wasn't possible.

What was he doing here?

Pia felt a sensation like emotional vertigo.

Hawk looked relaxed and at home in a green T-shirt and khakis, as casual as she'd ever seen him. He looked, in fact, as if he might have sauntered in after watching some television or grabbing a bite to eat in another part of the house.

Pia glanced at Lucy, bewildered.

"Have you met my brother, James Carsdale?" Lucy said with an inviting smile, seemingly unaware of anything untoward happening.

Lucy cast her brother an impish grin. "Do I need to recite all your titles, or will it suffice to enlighten Pia that you're also known as His Grace, the Duke of Hawkshire?"

"Carsdale?" Pia repeated, still forcing herself to focus on Lucy. "I thought your surname was Montgomery."

"Pia knows I have a title," Hawk said at the same time.

It was Lucy's turn to look perplexed. She glanced between her brother and Pia. "I feel as if I've walked in during the middle of the second act. Is there something I should know?"

Pia swung to look at Lucy. "Your brother and I are—" she spared Hawk a withering look "—acquainted."

Hawk arched a brow. "Well-acquainted."

"Past tense," Pia retorted.

"Obviously—on all counts," Lucy put in before turning to look at her brother. "You didn't tell me that you knew Pia. You suggested only that, on good authority, you had the name of an excellent wedding planner whom you wanted to recommend to me."

"The truth," Hawk responded.

Lucy arched a brow. "I take it *the good authority* was none other than yourself?"

Hawk inclined his head in silent acknowledgment, a mocking look in his eyes as they met Pia's.

"Yes," Pia put in acidly, "your brother is practiced in making the artful omission."

Lucy looked with interest from her brother to Pia and back. "On the stage, this would be called a moment of high drama," she quipped. "And here I thought, Hawk, that I had a lock on the thespian skills in the family."

Pia stood and reached for her handbag. "Thank you for the offer of tea, Lucy, but I won't be staying."

As Pia tried to step by Hawk on the way to the door, he took hold of her elbow, and she froze.

It was the first time he had touched her in three years— since the night they had first met. And despite herself, she couldn't help feeling Hawk's casual touch on her elbow to the tips of her toes. Her skin prickled at his nearness.

Why, oh why, did she have to remain so responsive to him?

Pia forced herself to look up. It was at a moment such as

this that she rued her lack of stature. And Hawk bested her on all counts...physical height, bearing and consequence in the world.

"I see you have the knack of anticipating requests," he said smoothly. "It's a useful skill in a wedding planner. And, as it happens, I was going to ask for a private word."

Fortunately, she regained some of her combativeness at his words, and she fumed silently even as she let Hawk guide her out the door to the parlor without protest. She was headed in that direction anyway and there was no use making a scene in front of his sister.

Once in the hall, however, she pulled away from Hawk's loose hold. "If you would summon your butler or majordomo, or whatever you call him, for my coat, I'll be on my way and we'll put an end to this charade of an interview."

"No," Hawk responded, pulling shut the parlor door.

"No?" *The gall...the utter nerve.*

Hawk smiled grimly. "Why pass up the chance to tell me, again, what you think of me? Or better yet, say it with finger food?" He nodded toward the room they'd just exited. "I noticed at least a few good scones in there."

"I'll permit Lucy to enjoy them."

"What a relief."

Her gaze clashed with his.

"It seems we're at an impasse," Hawk said dryly. "I refuse to let you leave with your coat until we've spoken, and you're—" he looked at a nearby window and the steady drizzle coming down "—determined to get wet."

"You're all wet," she retorted. "And for your information, I have a compact umbrella with me in my handbag."

Hawk sighed. "We can do this the hard way, and perhaps make a scene that Lucy will overhear, or we can retire to somewhere with a bit more privacy."

"You leave me little choice," Pia tossed back, her chin set at a mutinous angle.

Without waiting for a further invitation, Hawk steered her into a room across the hall.

As Hawk shut the door behind them, Pia noted that this room was unmistakably a library or study. It had built-in bookshelves, a marble mantel as impressive as the one in the parlor, and a large desk set in front of high windows. With plenty of dark, leather-upholstered furniture, the room was clearly Hawk's domain.

Pia turned back to confront Hawk. "I had no idea Lucy was related to you. She gave her name as Lucy Montgomery. Otherwise—"

"—you'd never have come?" he finished for her, his tone sardonic.

"Naturally."

"Montgomery is the stage name that Lucy adopted. It is, however, also a surname that appears in our family tree."

Pia raised her eyebrows. "Do all you Carsdales operate under a variety of names?"

"When it suits."

"And I suppose it suits when you're intent on seduction?"

She'd intended the comment as a sharp riposte, but he had the audacity to give her a slow, sensuous smile.

"Is that what it was—seduction?" he murmured. "To which you fell victim?"

"Through foul means."

"But still you were seduced by the man…not the title."

Pia detected a note of naked honesty in Hawk's banter, but she didn't let herself dwell on it. She didn't let herself dwell on anything—including the fact that they were in his library alone together—except holding on to her outrage.

"You masterminded this," she accused, looking around them. "You arranged to have me come here when you knew I was not suspecting…not ex-expecting…"

Words deserted her.

"It's not a charade, however," Hawk countered. "How could

it be? My sister needs to move up her wedding date, and you're a wedding consultant, last I heard."

"You know what I mean!"

"Does it matter if you can use the business?" Hawk replied.

Pia's eyes widened. "I don't know what you mean. In any case, I'm not that desperate."

"Aren't you?" Hawk said. "You've dropped hints that you've been less than busy lately."

Pia's eyes widened further.

"Never play poker."

"Seeking to make amends?"

"In a sense."

Pia placed her hands on her hips, contemplating him and his vague response. It *couldn't be* that he was feeling guilty about his behavior toward her in the past. He was a seasoned player who had forgotten her easily. That much was clear from the *three years* it had taken for their paths to cross again.

There was only one other possibility, then, for his motivation in linking her to Lucy.

"I suppose you feel some sense of responsibility since it was your friend who torpedoed my professional standing by ruining Belinda's wedding?" she asked.

Hawk hesitated, and then inclined his head. "I suppose *responsibility* is as good a term as any."

Pia eyed him. He was holding out a lifeline to her business, and it was hard not to grasp hold of the opportunity that he was offering. What better way to signal to society that all was well than to be hired to organize the wedding of the sister of the man whom she'd bearded with baba ghanoush?

She was being foolhardy.

"Lucy isn't part of New York society, but her future husband's family is," Hawk cajoled, as if sensing her weakness. "This wedding could help establish you. And Lucy has many ties to the theater world. I'm betting you've never planned a wedding for an actress before?"

Pia shook her head.

"Then Lucy's wedding will let you tap into a whole new market for your services."

"Wh-who would be employing me?"

She hated herself for asking—and hated herself more for stammering—but the question came out of its own volition. Rather than appear satisfied, however, Hawk's expression turned into a study of harmlessness.

"I'd be employing you, but only as a minor, technical detail."

"Minor to you."

"I'm the head of the family, and Lucy is young—only twenty-four." Hawk's lips twitched. "It seems only fair that I support her bid to remove herself from under the imposing family umbrella. Lucy was an unexpected bonus for my parents more than a decade after my mother delivered the heir and the spare."

Pia noted that Hawk had deftly turned an act that might be viewed as generous and loving on his part into a statement of sardonic self-deprecation.

She started to waver. She *had* liked Hawk's sister even on the basis of a very brief acquaintance. She felt a natural affinity for Lucy. It had deepened on learning that Hawk's sister was only three years younger than she was. Lucy was, in fact, the same age that Pia had been when she'd first met Hawk.

If her own tale with Hawk wasn't destined to have a happy ending, then at least she could see to it that one Carsdale…

No, she wouldn't let herself think of matters in that vein.

"You'll be dealing with Lucy mostly, obviously," Hawk continued, his expression open and unmasked. "I'll try to make myself as unobtrusive as possible."

"H-how?" Pia asked. "Are you planning to sequester yourself at your country estate in England?"

"Nothing so drastic," Hawk replied with amusement, "but, rest assured, I have no interest in weddings."

"Obviously—judging from your past behavior."

"Ouch." He had the grace to look abashed. "I stepped right into that comment, and I suppose I deserved it."

She raised her eyebrows and said nothing.

"The town house belongs to me," Hawk went on unperturbed, "but Lucy has had the run of it since I haven't been in regular residence until recently. And though I'm based in New York, rather than London, for business at the moment, I expect that my corporate dealings will still mean I'm not much at home."

Pia knew all about Hawk's hedge fund, of course. She'd read about it online. The success of his company over the past three years had raised his reputation to that of a first-class financier.

Darn. He must have women throwing themselves at him.

Not that she was interested, of course.

Pia wondered why Hawk was at home now, actually. The thought had occurred to her earlier, too—the minute he'd walked into the parlor. It could only be that he'd chosen to come into her meeting with Lucy, possibly betting that once she said yes to his sister, it would be best to reveal his connection to Lucy sooner rather than later.

Hawk arched an eyebrow. "And so…?"

Pia regarded him.

"I make you nervous, don't I?"

"N-naturally. I have a fear of snakes."

He grinned, unabashed.

"The endearing hiccup in your speech tells me everything I need to know about how much I affect you," he said, his voice smooth as silk and doubly seductive.

Pia felt a shiver of awareness chase down her spine for a

moment, but then Hawk's face changed to one as innocuous as a Boy Scout's.

"Of course," he went on solemnly, "we'll say no more on that topic. I plan to be on my best behavior from now on."

"Promise? Really?" she parried.

Before Hawk could reply, the library door opened. Lucy stuck her head inside, and then walked in when it was clear that she'd found them.

"Ah, there you are," Lucy said. "I was wondering if you'd run off, Pia."

"Nothing so drastic," Hawk responded mildly. "Pia and I were just discussing the terms of her employment."

Lucy looked at Pia with some surprise, and then clasped her hands together in delight. "You've agreed? Splendid!"

"I—"

"The hot water has gotten cold, but I'll order another pot for tea," Lucy said. "Shall we all return to the parlor?"

"Yes, let's," Hawk responded, his lips twitching.

As Pia followed Lucy from the room, and Hawk fell into step behind her, she was left to wonder if all the Carsdales had the gift of polite and subtle railroading.

For despite everything, she was finding herself agreeing to be Lucy's bridal consultant.

When Hawk emerged from the elevator, he had no trouble locating Pia's place. She'd opened her front door and was standing in the entrance to her apartment.

She looked fresh as a daisy in a yellow-print knit dress that displayed her lithe, compact body to perfection. The cleavage visible at the V-neck was just enough to give a man interesting thoughts.

He wondered whether he would always experience a quick jolt of sexual awareness when he saw her.

"How did you find me?" she asked without preamble.

He gave a careless shrug. "A little digging on Pia Lumley Wedding Productions. It wasn't hard."

Pia, he'd discovered, now lived on the fifth floor of a modest white-brick doorman building. The older man downstairs— more guard than doorman—had glanced up from his small television set long enough to ring Pia and announce Hawk's arrival. Even though Hawk had been privy only to a brief one-sided conversation—and from the guard's end at that— he'd sensed Pia's hesitancy when she'd been informed of his unexpected arrival. Still, moments later, he'd been directed to the elevator, and then the guard had gone back to viewing his talk show.

"Naturally," Pia responded now with a touch of sarcasm. "I should have expected you'd do some digging of your own. With a business, I'm easy to find, whether I like it or not."

Despite her words, she stepped aside to let him into the apartment, and then shut the door once he'd entered.

"In a way, I'm glad you're here," she said as he turned back to face her. "It makes matters easier."

He quirked a brow. "Only *in a way?*" he queried with dry amusement. "I suppose I should be happy there is at least one way."

"I've been having second thoughts."

"Of course you have." He let his mouth tilt upward. "And that's why *I'm* glad I'm here."

Hawk watched as Pia sucked in a deep breath and squared her shoulders.

"I'm afraid it wouldn't be wise for me to accept the job as Lucy's wedding planner."

"She'll be devastated."

"I'll find a suitable replacement."

"A rival?" he questioned sardonically. "Are you sure you want to?"

"I have contacts—friends."

"And I'm not one of them, presumably."

Hawk glanced around. The apartment wasn't big, but nevertheless bigger than he expected.

The living room was dressed in a pastel theme, from the peach-colored couch to the rose-print armchair. *Wedding colors.*

Binders of various wedding vendors—for invitations, decorations, flowers and more—stood out on the cream-colored bookshelves.

He glanced down as a cat sauntered in from an adjoining room.

The animal stopped, returned his stare, still as a statue, and then blinked.

"Mr. Darcy," Pia announced.

But of course, Hawk thought. A wedding planner with a cat named after Jane Austen's most renowned hero.

Hawk's lips twisted. Pia had wound up with Mr. Darcy, so all should be right with the world. Except Mr. Darcy was a damn cat, and Hawk surmised that *he'd* been cast as the villainous Mr. Wickham in this drama.

Still, he bent and rubbed the cat behind the ears. The feline allowed the contact and then moved to rub himself against Hawk's leg, leaving behind a trail of stray animal hairs on Hawk's pants.

When Hawk straightened, he caught Pia's look of surprise.

"What?" he asked. "You look astonished that I'd cozy up to your cat."

"I thought you would be a dog person," Pia responded. "Aren't all of you aristocrats fond of canines? Fox hunting and such?"

Hawk smiled. "Afraid I'd feed Puss 'n Boots here to the dogs?"

"The possibility wouldn't bear thinking about except that you've already proven yourself to be a wolf in sheep's clothing," Pia retorted.

He gave a feral grin and then, just to annoy her, allowed his gaze to travel over her. "And are you Little Red Riding Hood? Is that the fairy tale you prefer these days?"

"I don't prefer any fairy tales," she shot back. "N-not anymore."

Hawk's smile faded. She didn't believe in fairy tales anymore, and he felt responsible for robbing her of her innocence in more ways than one.

Of course, all that made it even more imperative that he change her mind and get her to accept his help. He intended to make restitution of sorts.

He pulled some papers from the inside pocket of his blazer. "I suspected that you might have a change of heart once you had a chance to think about what you were getting into with Lucy."

"You were the one who wanted time to review the contract!" she accused. "I'm within my rights to change my mind, and if you don't have any recourse, you have only yourself to blame."

It was true that when Pia had handed Lucy her standard written wedding services contract on Monday, before she'd left Hawk's house, he'd taken the contract in hand and had asked to review it. But only because he'd thought it would give him another opportunity to interact with her when he brought it back to her.

He'd come here this afternoon directly from work, and was still wearing a navy business suit.

The discussion of the contract, he told himself, would afford him a chance to change her low opinion of him. Maybe he could begin to demonstrate that he wasn't quite the reprobate she thought he was. Not anymore.

"I did do as I said," he acknowledged, unfolding the paper in his hand. "I did review it."

Pia arched a brow. "One wonders why you don't bring

the same thoroughness and discrimination to your choice of dates."

Hawk stifled the dry chuckle that rose unbidden. "You've done some research on me, I take it."

Pia nodded. "The internet is a wonderful thing. I believe you were referred to on at least one occasion as Jolly Lord James, his Rollicking Rowdy Ruffianness?"

"Ruffian?" Hawk rubbed the bridge of his nose with his finger. "Ah, yes, I believe I had my nose broken at least once in a brawl. A useful thing once I became Hawkshire, as I was able to live up to the profile implied."

"Charming."

"And did your research also reveal how I succeeded to the title of Duke of Hawkshire?" he asked with deceptive casualness.

Pia shook her head. "I believe the tabloids were already fully occupied with your ne'er-do-well travails."

"So I've heard," he deadpanned. "Much to my regret, however, my sojourn as the rollicking younger son of the previous Duke of Hawkshire was cut short when my older brother died from injuries sustained in a boating accident."

He saw Pia hesitate.

"An early morning phone call awakened me from a pleasant slumber, as I recall," he went on, searching her gaze. "I still remember the view from your apartment window as the news reached me."

Pia looked momentarily bewildered. He knew he'd flummoxed her.

"So you departed without a word?"

He nodded. "On the first flight back to London."

The unexpected news about his brother had changed the trajectory of his life. He'd left Pia's apartment quietly, while she'd still slept. Then he'd rushed back to London for a bedside vigil that had ended days later when William had taken his last breath.

With the tumult in his life that had followed the tragedy, he'd been able to push Pia to the back of his mind. Then with the space of days and miles, and the weight of his newfound responsibilities as a ducal heir, he convinced himself that it would be better if he didn't get in touch with her again—if he let matters end as they were.

It had all been convenient, too, he admitted to himself now. Because the truth was that after sleeping with Pia and discovering that she'd been a virgin, he'd had the feeling of being in too deep. It had been a novel and uncomfortable sensation for him. His younger, inconsiderate self had simply been looking for a steamy fling. But he'd been spared the need to figure out how to handle it all by the news of his brother's tragic accident.

"I'm sorry, however belatedly, for your loss," Pia said, a look of openhearted feeling transforming her face.

"I'm not asking for your sympathy," he responded.

He didn't deserve it. As much as Pia had claimed to have developed a more cynical shell since they'd been lovers, she still, he could tell, possessed a soft-hearted fragility about her that showed how easily she could be hurt.

He was thankful for that sign that he hadn't changed her too deeply, even though it made her all that more dangerous. *To him.*

He was here to help, he reminded himself. He was going to make amends for past wrongs, however inadequately, and that's all.

"My father died months later," he elaborated, forcing himself to stay on topic. "Some would say brokenhearted, though he'd already been in poor health. So by two quirks of fate within a year, I became the duke."

"And then you started Sunhill Investments," Pia observed without inflection. "You've had a busy few years."

He inclined his head. "Again, some would say so. And yet it was all born of necessity, and nothing more so than the need to find a new cash flow for the maintenance of the ducal estates."

When his father had died, the full weight of the dukedom had been thrust upon his shoulders. He'd stepped up to take care of the family...become responsible...

He'd already started exploring his options for starting a hedge fund, but the costs associated with the ducal estates had added new urgency to matters.

And in the shuffle—in the crazy upheaval and burdensome work schedule that had been his life for the past three years—it had been easy to shut the door on his discomfort as far as Pia was concerned. He had, at many moments, been too busy to think about their one stupendous night, when he'd broken his vow and done what he said he'd never do, even in his careless playboy days—be remembered as a woman's first lover. And even in his younger days, he hadn't been the type to leave without a word—instead, he stuck around and made sure there were no hard feelings.

"You never got back in touch," Pia stated, though without rancor.

He searched her eyes—so unusual in their warm amber tone that he'd been arrested by them on their first meeting.

Now, he sensed in them that her adamancy from when he'd walked in the door was weakening, exactly as he'd wanted. Still, what he said next was the truth. "None of this explanation was intended as an excuse."

"Why go out of your way to arrange for me to be Lucy's wedding planner?" Pia asked. "To make amends?"

Hawk couldn't help but smile at her astute query. Pia might still be rather sweet and naive, despite her posturing to the contrary, but she was intelligent. He'd been drawn to her wit on the night they'd first met.

"If I said yes, would you let me?" he parried.

"I've found from past experience that letting you do anything is dangerous."

He gave a low laugh. "Even if it's a favor?"

"With no strings attached?"

He could sense her weakening toward him, so he gave her his most innocent look. "Would you let me wipe some of the dirt off my conscience?"

"So this is an act of mercy on my part?"

"Of sorts."

"So you're acting not only to make up for your friend Easterbridge's actions at Belinda's wedding but for yours in the past as well?"

"I don't believe I was ever motivated by Easterbridge's actions."

Then, not giving her a chance to backtrack, he withdrew a pen from his inner jacket pocket and using the nearby wall as support, he inked her contract with his signature.

"There, it's signed," he said, handing out the contract to her.

She looked at him with some wariness, but nevertheless took the contract from him and glanced at it.

"Hawkshire," she read, and then looked up, a sudden glimmer in her eyes. "How grand. Sh-should I receive it as a benediction of sorts?"

He shrugged, willing for her to be amused at his expense. "Am I being permitted to try to make restitution, however inadequately? Then please view this contract as a grant of clemency from you to me."

Deliberately, he held the pen out to her.

Pia seemed to understand his gesture for the meaning-laden act it was, and hesitated.

Hawk glanced down at Mr. Darcy for a moment, and then arched a brow. "Our one witness wants you to sign."

And indeed, Mr. Darcy was looking up at them, unmoving and unblinking. Hawk was starting to realize that it was a customary pose for the cat, and he got the uncomfortable feeling that Mr. Darcy understood too much for a feline.

"I'm not in the business of reforming rakes," Pia said as she reached for the pen.

Their fingers brushed, causing a sizzle of awareness to shoot through him.

Hawk schooled his expression. "Of course you are," he contradicted her. "I assume you adopted Mr. Darcy from a shelter?"

"That was saving a soul, not reforming a rake."

"Is there much difference?" he asked. "And anyway, who knows what dastardly deeds and reprobate behavior Mr. Darcy engaged in before you met him?"

"Better the devil you don't know," she responded, turning a well-known saying on its head.

He placed his hand over his heart. "And yet one could say we encountered each other under blind circumstances not so different from your first meeting with Mr. Darcy. Surely, if you can find it in your heart to take him…?"

"I am not taking you in like…a-a stray," she responded reprovingly.

"Much to my regret," he murmured.

Giving him a lingering cautionary look, she turned her back and, using the wall for support in imitation of his earlier action, signed the contract.

She turned back to him and handed him a copy of the contract.

"Splendid," he said with a grin. "I'd kiss you to seal the deal, but I'll venture to guess you wouldn't find it appropriate under the circumstances."

"Certainly not!"

"A handshake then?"

Pia eyed him, and he returned her regard with a bland look of his own.

Slowly, she extended her hand, and he grasped it in his.

He let himself feel the vibrant current coursing between

them. It was the same as when they'd met three years ago. It was the same as it always was.

Her hand was small and fine-boned. The fingers, he'd noticed, tapered to well-manicured nails that nevertheless showed not a hint of polish—so like her, delicate but practical.

When she tried to pull away, he tightened his hold, drawing out the contact for reasons he didn't bother to examine.

She looked up at him questioningly, and he read the turbulent sexual awareness in her amber eyes.

In a courtly gesture, he bent and gave her a very proper kiss on the hand.

He heard Pia suck in a breath, and as he straightened, he released her hand.

She swallowed. "Why did you do that?"

"I'm a duke," he said, the excuse falling easily from his lips. "It's a done thing."

In fact, Hawk admitted to himself, the context wasn't fitting even if the gesture might have been. He wasn't greeting a woman—one of higher social status—who'd offered him her hand. But he brushed aside those niceties, not least because it had been tempting to touch her.

"Of course," Pia acknowledged lightly, though a shadow crossed her face. "I know all about your world, even if I'm not part of it."

"You've agreed to be part of it now," he countered. "Attend the theater with me tomorrow night."

"Wh-what?" she asked, looking startled. "Why?"

He smiled. "It's Lucy's off-Broadway show. Seeing my sister on the stage, in her element, might give you useful insight into her personality."

Pia relaxed her shoulders.

He could tell she'd been wondering whether he was reneging on his promise even before the ink had dried on their contract. Was he trying to entice her back into his bed?

Yes—*no. No.* He corrected the response that had jumped unbidden into his head. Fortunately, he hadn't spoken aloud.

Nevertheless, Pia seemed ready to argue. "I don't think a show would be—"

"—the ticket?" he finished. "Don't worry about it. I've got two seats in the front orchestra." He winked. "I worked the family connection."

"You know what I mean!"

"Hardly. And that seems to be a recurring problem of mine."

Pia looked as if she wanted to continue to protest.

"I'll see you tomorrow night. I'll come by at seven." He glanced down at the cat. "I hope Mr. Darcy won't mind spending the evening at home alone."

"Why?" she jabbed, but lightly. "Is he an uncomfortable reminder that the role left to you might be that of villain?"

He felt the side of his mouth tease upward. "How did you guess?"

Pia raised her eyebrows, but the look she gave him was open and unguarded.

"I'm not too concerned."

"Oh?"

He glanced down at Mr. Darcy again. "I feel confident that only one of us can waltz."

"Oh."

Pia looked startled and then, for a moment, dreamy—as if the idea of a waltz had called to the romantic in her.

Mr. Darcy just continued to stare at them unblinkingly, and Hawk realized that now was as good a time as any for him to leave, before he gave in to too much temptation.

He let the side of his mouth quirk up again. "Since I appear to have exhausted my options for acceptable salutations and social niceties, I'm afraid my goodbye will have to be rather dull."

"How reassuring," Pia answered, recovering.

He touched his finger to the tip of her pert nose in humorous salute of her impertinence.

And then, unable to stop himself, he let his finger wander down and smooth over her pink and inviting lips.

They both quieted.

"Tomorrow night," he repeated.

He turned away before he was tempted to touch her lips with his, and then let himself out the way he'd come in.

As he pulled shut the apartment door behind him, Hawk refused to let himself think about why he found it hard to leave Pia.

It was a vexing situation that could only mean no good for his best of intentions.

Five

Pia found herself staring at her apartment door after Hawk had left. Flooded with conflicting emotions, she hugged herself and sat down on her couch.

She touched her fingers to her lips, in imitation of Hawk's action moments ago. She could swear he'd wanted to kiss her. The last time he'd kissed her had been on the night that they'd first met....

Pia turned away and picked up the remote to her MP3 player because music relaxed her. Within a few moments, the dulcet tones of an orchestral ensemble drifted through the apartment from her small speakers.

"W-would you like a drink?" she asked.

James laughed close behind her. "What a question to ask, considering we've just been to a bar."

In truth, she felt light-headed herself. It must have been that last cocktail she'd had at the bar while trying to converse with the real estate office manager.

"Pia," James said quietly, laying his hands on her shoulders.
She froze at the contact, her nipples tightening.

"Relax," he murmured close to her ear.

Oh.

He removed his hands…but moments later, she felt his fingertips trail up her arms as he nuzzled the hair near her ear.

She shivered. "Really, I—"

He nipped her earlobe.

She gulped, and then forced herself to say, "D-don't you want to get to know each other better?"

"Much better," he agreed on a soft laugh.

His body brushed hers from behind, sending delicious shivers through her.

Slowly, he turned her to face him, and then searched her eyes. "I've been wanting to do this—" he bent and tasted her lips "—ever since we left the bar."

"Oh," she breathed.

This was her fantasy. *He was here now.*

He cupped her shoulders, his thumbs tracing a soothing circular pattern. "We won't do anything you don't want to do."

"Th-that's what I'm afraid of."

He smiled. "Ah, Pia. You really are special." Then his expression turned more intent and amorous. "Let me show you how much."

He cupped her cheek, laid his lips against hers and tasted her.

She sighed and gripped his shirt, fisting her hand into the material, as little shock waves of pleasure jolted her.

She felt his arousal grow between them as his mouth stroked hers. Within moments, they had fitted their bodies together, giving in to the desire that had been kindled in the bar and stoked on the cab ride to her apartment.

He cupped her face with both hands, his fingers delving into her hair as he sipped from her mouth.

She relaxed her grip on his shirt and flattened her hands against his chest, where she could feel the steady beat of his heart.

Around them, the sweet notes of string instruments sounded, the tune low and soulful.

Pia felt herself relax even as every inch of her skin tingled with awareness. She sighed against James's mouth, wanting the kiss to go on and on as his hunger matched her own.

Giving in to the urge to shed attire, she kicked off her sandals. In the next moment, she lowered a couple of inches, enough to break the contact of her lips with James's.

"My bed isn't very big." They were the first words to pop out of her mouth, her tone apologetic, and she flushed.

James looked indulgent, and then dimpled as he nodded beside them. "You've never made love on a love seat before?"

She'd never made love *period*. But she was afraid if she told him, he'd flee out the door. She knew he must be used to more experienced women.

She shrugged one shoulder. "Why bother when a bed is available?"

"Mmm," he said, and then bent and nuzzled her ear.

Oh. She gripped his upper arms for support, her fingers digging into his biceps, as his action did funny things to her insides.

She felt his hand go to the zipper at the back of her dress.

"Would it be okay if I did this?" he murmured.

"Yes, please," she breathed.

She heard the rasp of the zipper and felt her dress slither downward, exposing to his gaze that she wasn't wearing a bra.

James stepped back and looked at her with a hooded, rapt expression.

"Ah, Pia, you're so beautiful." He raised his hands to cup

and caress her. "You're just as pretty as I thought when my imagination was running rampant in the bar."

"Kiss me," she whispered.

He sat on the arm of the love seat beside them and, pulling her toward him, fastened his mouth over one pert breast.

Pia was lost. Her heart beat wildly, and she tangled her fingers in his hair.

He pushed the rest of the dress off her, and then peeled her panties away without lifting his mouth from her.

Pia moaned.

He shifted his focus to her other breast, but then paused, his lips hovering over her taut flesh, his breath fanning her erect nipple.

"And would it be okay if I kissed you here?" he said hoarsely.

Pia had never been so close to begging and pleading.

But instead of answering, she guided his head to her breast, her eyes fluttering shut on a sigh as his lips closed over her.

He soothed and aroused her with his tongue, fanning the fire of their desire.

Before she knew it, she was on his lap on the love seat, and they were kissing passionately but yet like longtime lovers who had all the time in the world. His arousal pressed against her flesh, and his hand caressed up and down her thigh.

When they finally broke away, he groaned softly. "Have mercy, Pia."

In response, she snuggled closer. He nuzzled her temple and his breath rasped in her ear. She shivered and rubbed against him.

She let her hand go to the buttons of his shirt, undoing one and then another. The strong, corded line of his neck came into view.

"Pia," he said from somewhere above her head, "please say you don't want to stop."

"Who said anything about stopping?" This was her

fantasy, and she found that she wanted to see it through to its conclusion. Her last drink at the bar had given her a delicious, unbound feeling, and James's seduction had lowered her inhibitions even more.

"Ah, Pia." He slipped his hand between her thighs and pressed, giving her a heady sensation. "I just want to assure you that I'm clean."

"I am, too," she answered, understanding what he was alluding to. "I've never had unprotected sex."

It was literally true, though it hid the truth—that she'd never had sex at all.

He kissed her neck. "Are you...? If not, I have something with me. Not that I walked in here with any expectations, of course, but I'd be lying if I said I wasn't attracted to you from the first moment I spotted you."

"Mmm...when did you first notice me? Are you saying our encounter in the bar wasn't by chance?"

"I saw you minutes before you tried to order a drink," he admitted. "When I spotted a damsel in distress, though, I saw my opening. I took a chance that Cinderella was looking for a Prince Charming to come rescue her, and that she'd mistake me for him if I tried to do her a favor."

Pia's heart gave a little squeeze. It was as if he knew her well already. Did he suspect that she was a romantic at heart? Did he know that she'd thrilled to stories of true love, though a part of her knew better?

She pulled his head down for a kiss as the music reached a low crescendo around them.

They kissed deeply, their mouths clinging, unable to get enough of each other.

When he finally broke their kiss, he stood up with her in his arms. "What's your preference, Cinderella?"

She glanced down at the love seat—next time.

"Bed," she said.

"My sentiments exactly," he said, and then strode with her

around the partition to where the bed was. "See, we have a lot in common."

"Besides riding and fishing?"

He paused in the act of placing her on the bed. "Oh, Pia, sweetheart," he said huskily, a wicked glimmer in his eye, "isn't that what tonight is all about—fishing and riding?"

Pia felt a full-body flush sweep over her. As she came down on the mattress, she propped herself up on her elbows to stop from lying completely on her back.

She swallowed, unable to say anything.

Holding her eyes, James undid the remaining buttons on his shirt and cuffs, and then pulled fabric from his waistband, stripping off his shirt and undershirt.

Pia soaked up the sight of him. Taut muscle rippled underneath the planes of smooth and lightly tanned skin.

She hadn't been mistaken. He was fit and in top shape.

He made short work of the rest of his clothes, working methodically until he was naked.

His arousal stood in imposing relief against his toned frame.

Pia sucked in a breath. "You're very beautiful."

James gave her a lopsided smile. "Isn't that my line?"

It occurred to her that while she'd viewed pictures of naked men, this was the first time she'd seen one in the flesh. And again, James was beyond her expectations. He was impressive—tall and built as well as fit. The flat planes of his abdomen tapered down to…a definite sign that he wanted to couple with her. *Right now.*

A tingle went through her, a tightening of anticipation.

As if in response, he pulled her toward him on the bed and began kissing his way down her body.

Pia looked up at the white plaster ceiling, her hands tangling in his hair, and thought she'd die of pleasure.

James kissed the jut of her hip and then worked his way down the soft skin of her inner thigh to the sensitive spot behind her knee. He lifted her other leg and turned his head to nip and brush the pliant flesh of her other thigh.

With one finger, he traced down the cleft at the juncture of her thighs, and she moaned, her head twisting until she pressed her face into the coverlet beside her.

James muttered sweet encouragement as he lowered her leg and caressed his hand down her thigh.

Then he bent, picked up his pants from the floor and fished out a packet of protection. He donned the sheath with economical moves. Stretching out beside her on the bed, he gathered her to him and soothed her with his lips and hands as he muttered soft endearments under his breath.

Pia was lost to the sensation and emotion sweeping her. She was petite and felt surrounded by him.

When James shifted over her, parting her thighs and settling against her, she worried about being able to accept him. But within seconds she was again consumed by the desire flaring between them.

"Touch me, Pia," he said hoarsely.

He sipped and feasted on her lips, his hands readying her with a gentle kneading. Pia responded in kind, meeting his mouth and trailing her fingertips over the corded muscles of his back.

This was the moment she'd waited a lifetime for. *He* was the man she'd waited for.

James nudged her, and Pia concentrated on relaxing as he sucked on her lower lip.

Lifting his head, he muttered, "Wrap your legs around me."

Oh, sweet heaven. She'd never been plastered, open and exposed, to an aroused male before.

She concentrated on what she'd imagined countless times in her fantasies, where her partner's features had always been indistinct but he'd carried an aura so very much like James's.

She did as he instructed, and James grasped her hips in his hands.

He looked deeply into her eyes and then gave her a quick, gentle kiss.

"Let me take you, Pia," he said throatily. "Let me bring you pleasure."

She arched toward him, and in response, he buried his head in her neck and penetrated her.

Pia gasped, and then bit down hard on her lip.

James froze.

Moments passed and they held still. The thumping of his heart sounded against hers.

He lifted his head, his expression puzzled, and also shocked and doubtful.

"You're a virgin."

He stated it with surprise.

She wet her lips. "W-was. I think past tense is appropriate."

She felt full and stretched, almost to the point of the unbearable, where pleasure met pain. It was a strange sensation that she tried to get used to.

"Why?"

She swallowed, and then whispered, "I wanted you. Is that so bad?"

James closed his eyes, his muscles remaining full of tension as he rested his forehead against hers and then muttered a self-deprecation. "You're so unbelievably tight and hot. Sweet like I've never experienced… Pia, I can't—"

Afraid he'd pull out, she clamped her legs around him. "D-don't."

After a moment, some of the tension eased out of him— almost as if he was reluctantly admitting defeat.

"I'll try to make it good for you from now on," he muttered, as if the words were torn from him.

"Yes."

He moved slowly then, his hands pressing the right spots and easing the tension in her body.

Pia focused on relaxing and concentrated on the sensation of his movements.

Slowly, slowly, she felt a small spark, and then a faint tingle. She was awakening, her body coming to life under his sure ministrations.

Eventually, as she relaxed further, tension built. She felt herself reaching for a release that she'd never experienced with a man before.

James stroked between their bodies, his fingers pressing on her most sensitive spot.

Within moments, she cried out with pleasure and then crested before she knew it. She was carried on a wave of sensation as feeling after feeling swamped her.

Her body undulated around James of its own accord, massaging him into his own frenzy of need.

"Have mercy, Pia," he groaned.

It was too late, however. With a hoarse oath, he grasped her hips and pumped into her.

She came for him again. And then with a final thrust, he took his own release.

As James slumped against her, Pia hugged him and suddenly became aware of tears in her eyes.

He'd taken her across the final barrier to realizing herself sexually as a woman. Their joining and her first time couldn't have been more wonderful.

Pia closed her eyes, and of their own accord, exhaustion and sleep claimed her.

The next time she blinked up at her ceiling, he was gone.

In a moment, Pia was brought back to the present. She realized she wasn't staring at her ceiling, but at her apartment wall.

Different apartments, three years apart.

Same man, though.

Hawk.

His presence was palpable still, and her body was awakened and aware as if they'd made love moments, not years, ago.

Pia shook her head. *No.*

She'd let him into her sanctuary—her apartment—again, but she resolved not to let him into her life one more time.

The night after Hawk signed the contract at her apartment, Pia discovered they had a couple of the best theater seats in the house—no doubt thanks to Hawk's personal connection.

Hawk had appeared at her apartment at seven and driven them so they could make the eight o'clock curtain call for Lucy's show, an off-Broadway production of the musical *Oklahoma,* in which Lucy had a supporting role.

Pia made a show of studying her program as they waited for the lights to dim. Tonight, she reminded herself, was all about business. She'd dressed in a short-sleeved, apricot-colored dress that she'd worn to work-related parties before and that she hoped sent the appropriate message. She'd avoided those items in her wardrobe that she considered purely off-hours attire.

She stole a quick sidelong glance at Hawk, who was looking at the stage. Even dressed casually in black pants and a light blue shirt, he managed to project an air of ducal self-possession.

She just wished she wasn't so aware of his thigh inches away from her own, and of his shoulder and arm within dangerously close brushing distance. If there was a petition right now for having individual armrests in places of public accommodations, she'd sign on the spot.

Determinedly, she pulled herself in, making it clear that she'd cede the shared armrest to him.

In the process, she absently tugged down the hem of her dress, and Hawk's gaze was drawn to her actions.

As Hawk surveyed her exposed thighs, his expression changing to one of alert but lazy amusement, Pia rued her involuntary action.

Hawk's eyes moved up to meet hers. "I have a proposition for you."

"I-I'm not surprised," she shot back, rallying and cursing her telltale stammer. "They do appear to be your forte."

He had the indecency to grin. "You bring out the best—" he waited a beat as her eyes widened "—urges in me."

She hated that he could bait her so successfully. "You give me too much credit. As far as I can tell, your urges don't need any help in being called forth. They appear of their own volition."

Hawk chuckled. "Aren't you at least curious about what I have to offer?"

She frowned, but forced herself to adopt a saccharine-sweet voice. "You forget that I already know. Unless your offer involves business, I'm not interested."

Was his facility with sexual innuendo boundless?

He shifted toward her, his leg brushing her own, and Pia tried to stifle her response of frozen awareness before he could discern it.

Hawk looked too knowing. "As it happens, it does. Involve business, that is."

This time, Pia didn't try to hide her reaction. "It does?"

Hawk nodded. "A friend of mine, Victoria, needs help with a wedding."

"A female friend? Ready to give up on you, is she, and move on?"

She couldn't stop herself from needling him, it seemed.

He flashed a grin. "We never dated. Her fiancé is an old classmate of mine. I introduced them to each other at a party last year."

"You do seem to know quite a few people who are getting

married." She raised her eyebrows. "Always the matchmaker, never the groom?"

"Not yet," he replied cryptically.

She fell silent at his vague response.

Once upon a time, *he* might have featured in *her* wedding fantasies, but they were well past that point, weren't they? Instead of the well-trod path, they'd veered down a detour from which there was no turning back.

"When is the wedding?" she heard herself ask.

"Next week. Saturday."

"Next week?"

She wasn't sure she'd heard correctly.

Hawk nodded. "The wedding planner is quarantined abroad."

Pia raised her eyebrows.

Hawk quirked his lips. "I'm not joking. She went on safari with her boyfriend, and they were both exposed to tuberculosis. She can't get back to New York until after the wedding date."

Pia shook her head in bemusement. "I suppose I should thank you…?"

"If you want to," he teased. "It might be appropriate under the circumstances."

Pia bit her lip, but Hawk looked down and pulled out a piece of paper from his pocket.

"Here's the bride's contact information," he said. "Will you do it? Will you call her?"

Pia took the paper from him, her fingers brushing his in a contact that was anything but casual for the two of them.

She noted the name and phone number that he'd written. *Victoria Elgemere.*

Just then the lights overhead blinked a few times, indicating that people should take their seats because the show was about to begin.

"I'll call her," she said quickly.

"Good girl," Hawk responded, and then mischievously patted her knee, his hand lingering. "I'll be a wedding guest, by the way."

"Then it'll be déjà vu."

He grinned. "I've developed a taste for baba ghanoush."

She threw him a stern look, and then picked up and returned his hand to him. Her actions belied the emotional tumult that he so effortlessly engendered in her.

Facing forward as the lights dimmed, she was left to reflect that her company had again received a desperate transfusion of new business thanks to Hawk.

She'd acted quickly in accepting the job—or, at least, agreeing to call—forced into an impulsive decision by the imminent start of the show, but she didn't want her feelings toward him to get murky.

She could start feeling gratitude or worse.

Six

Hawk emerged from an Aston Martin at the New York Botanical Garden—where Victoria's wedding would shortly be held at four o'clock on a Saturday afternoon—and looked up.

He saw nothing but clear blue skies. There was just the faint hint of a warm breeze. *Perfect.*

As the valet approached for his car keys, Hawk heard his cell phone ring and smiled as the notes of "Unforgettable" by Nat King Cole sounded. He'd assigned the ringtone to Pia's cell, whose number he'd acquired ostensibly for business reasons.

He'd thought of using the theme music from *Jaws* for her ringtone, but then he figured that while it might be appropriate, given the sparring nature of his relationship with her, she didn't need further encouragement, if she ever found out, to attempt to annihilate him.

With a grin, he took the call.

"Hawk, where are you?" Pia demanded without preamble.

"I'm about to hand my cars keys to the valet," he responded. "Should I be anywhere else?"

"I'll be right there! The bride left her veil in the back of a Lincoln Town Car that departed minutes ago. I need your help."

"What…?"

"You heard me." Pia's voice held an edge of crisis. "Oh, I can't be associated with another wedding disaster!"

"You won't." *Not if he could help it*. "What's the name of the car service?"

As Pia gave it to him, Hawk shook his head at the valet and jumped back into his car to start the ignition.

"Call the car company," he told Pia, "and tell them to contact the driver."

"I already have. They're trying to get in touch with him. He can't go too far. Otherwise, we'll never get the veil back in time for the ceremony."

"Don't worry, I'm on it." He started to steer back down the drive with one hand. "Do you think he's heading back to Manhattan?"

If he had some idea in which direction the car was heading, he'd know which way to go once he got out of the Botanical Garden. Then when contact was made with the driver, at least he'd be nearby and they could meet at a convenient exit or intersection.

"I think he is heading south, and I'm coming with you," Pia replied.

"No, you're needed here."

"Look to your left. I'm heading toward you. Stop and I'll hop in."

Hawk turned to look out the driver's-side window. Sure enough, there was Pia, hurrying toward him across the grass, a phone pressed to her ear.

"Good grief, Pia." He disconnected the call and stopped the car.

Moments later, she pulled open the passenger-side door and slid inside.

As he pulled away again, he observed with amusement, "I don't think I've ever seen a woman so anxious to get into a car with me."

"It's an Aston Martin," she said, breathing heavily from her jog. "You can really accelerate, and I'm desperate."

"The first time I think I've been praised for my ability to go fast."

"J-just drive." She breathed in deep, then, pressing a button, put her phone to her ear once more.

Hawk assumed she was calling the car service again.

He glanced at her. She was wearing a short-sleeved caramel-color satin dress with a gently-flared skirt and matching tan kitten heels. He'd already identified the outfit as she was racing toward him as another of what he'd come to think of as her working-party dresses—festive but not so eye-catching that they'd detract attention from where it was meant to be.

Now he listened to her half of the conversation with the car service. It seemed as if she was getting good news.

In fact, when the call was over, Pia slumped with relief.

"They got through to the driver," she said. "He's getting off the highway and meeting us three exits away at a gas station rest stop."

"Great." *On to more enchanting matters.* He nodded to her dress. "You look nice."

She threw him a startled look, as if not expecting the compliment. "Thanks."

He felt a smile pull at his lips as he tossed her a sidelong look. "Do you pick your wedding clothes with an eye toward being able to make a quick sprint? You made good time across the grass. Rather impressive in those shoes."

"Weddings can be full of the unexpected," she replied. "You should know that as well as anyone."

He arched a brow. "Still, I'm curious. You phoned me to come to your rescue. Am I your modern-day knight riding to the rescue in a black sports car?"

"Hardly," she replied tartly. "There are very few people I know at this wedding, and you got me into this mess—"

He laughed.

"—so the least you could do when you arrived at just the right moment was to lend a set of wheels."

"Ah, of course."

He let the discussion go at that, though he was tempted to tease her some more.

Moments later, he took the highway exit that she indicated and found the gas station.

The driver of the car service was waiting for them, a shopping bag in hand.

After Pia took the errant veil from the driver and thanked him quickly, she and Hawk hopped back into his car.

"The day has been saved," Hawk remarked as he put the key back in the ignition.

"Not yet," Pia responded. "The wedding isn't over. Trust me on this one. I've been to more weddings than there are lights in Times Square."

"Yes, but isn't this the moment when you thank your hero with a kiss?"

She jerked to look at him, her eyes widening.

Not giving her a chance to think it over, he leaned forward and touched his lips to hers.

Lord, he thought, her lips were as pillowy soft as they looked. *Just as he remembered.*

Even though he knew he should stop, when he heard and felt Pia's breath hitch, he deepened the kiss, settling his lips more firmly on hers.

She didn't pull away, and he drew out the kiss, molding her lips with his. With his hand, he stroked the soft skin of her jaw and throat.

She relaxed and sighed, and leaned toward him. And it was all he could do not to draw her into an embrace and feed the desire between them.

He finally forced himself to pull back and look at her. "There…recompense received."

"I—I—" Pia cleared her throat and frowned. "You're quite the expert at stealing kisses, aren't you?"

Solemnly, he placed his hand over his heart. "It's a rare occasion that I have the opportunity to act so gallantly."

She hesitated, and then gave him a stern look and faced forward. "We need to get back."

They made it back to the New York Botanical Garden in record time while Pia filled him in with desultory wedding details.

When he pulled up in front of the valet again, Pia rushed away to help the bride. As Hawk dealt with the car and the valet again, he reflected that he'd heard nothing but good things from Victoria and Timothy about Pia's eleventh-hour help with their wedding. He was impressed by how professionally Pia had handled herself with little time to prepare.

After leaving the valet, Hawk sauntered alone toward the other guests mingling on the grassy outdoor space where the ceremony was to take place, surrounded by the Botanical Garden's rich greenery. The bridal arch and bedecked chairs, arranged by the florist, stood at the ready.

He made idle chitchat with some fellow guests, but within twenty minutes, everyone was seated and the ceremony started.

The bride looked pretty and the groom beamed, but Hawk only had eyes for Pia, standing discreetly to one side, within a few feet of the seat he'd chosen for himself in one of the back rows.

Suddenly catching Pia's eye, he motioned for her to take the empty seat next to him.

She hesitated for a moment, but then slipped into the white folding chair next to him.

Hawk smiled to himself. But as he stared ahead, watching the bride and groom, more weighty thoughts eventually intruded.

He'd chosen long ago to attend this wedding alone. Victoria and her groom, Timothy, were longtime friends of his, and he'd found that for this occasion at least, he wanted to be free of expectations. At his age, society and the press were apt to view any date of his as a potential duchess.

Hawk reflected that Victoria and Timothy were going through a rite of passage that would soon be expected of him. Tim was an Old Etonian, like him, and Victoria was a baron's daughter who had attended all the right schools and now had a socially acceptable job as the assistant to an up-and-coming British designer.

Victoria, in fact, had precisely the pedigree and background that would be expected for the bride of a duke. She was the sort of woman of whom his mother would approve.

Hawk's mind went to his mother's attempt at matchmaking with Michelene Ward-Fombley in particular, but he pushed the thought aside.

He stole a look at Pia next to him. Her business had trained her in the etiquette of the elite, but that couldn't change her background or give her connections that she didn't possess. With the crowd here today, she'd always be the bridal consultant, never the bride.

At that moment, Pia's lips parted as she looked to the front, and her expression became rather emotional.

Pia cried at weddings.

The thought flashed through Hawk's mind like a news bulletin and was closely followed by the realization that Pia was doing what she loved to do. Weddings, he realized, were more than a job to her.

He'd meant to make things up to her, in a way, by arranging for her to coordinate this wedding and Lucy's. But he'd also, in the process, tested the limits of their relationship because he enjoyed teasing her.

It had been too tempting to spar with her and watch her eyes flash. He admitted to himself that any reaction from Pia was better than having her treat him with indifference. And her kiss…it was hard to imagine a better reaction than that.

But the last thing he wanted to do was to hurt Pia again, he reminded himself. A relationship wouldn't be possible for them, and he shouldn't tease either of them with kisses that couldn't lead to anything more. She deserved to be able to get on with her life, and so did he.

A dog started barking, recalling him from his thoughts.

Beside him, Pia sat up straighter.

Hawk had noted before that the only surprising touch to the ceremony was the bride's King Charles Spaniel, who'd been dressed with an ivory collar and bow and had been led down the aisle by an attendant.

Now, he spotted the dog up front near the bridal arch, playing with—or rather, tearing at—a flower arrangement on the ground.

"Not the dog, please," Pia said under her breath. "We haven't even taken photos with the bridal bouquet yet."

Hawk glanced at her. At the beginning of the ceremony, he'd seen the bride place her flowers on a small pedestal. The pooch-cum-bridal attendant had somehow gotten hold of them.

Hawk couldn't remember the name of Victoria's canine. Finola? Feefee? In any case, *Trouble* seemed appropriate at the moment.

He watched as the bride knelt down, and then her dog sprinted away, bouquet in mouth.

So much for asking if anyone had any objections to this marriage...

"I have to do something," Pia muttered as she started to rise.

Hawk wasn't sure if Pia was talking to herself or to him, and if it mattered. He rose, too, and laid a staying hand on Pia's wrist. "Forget it. In those heels, you'll never catch—"

"Finola."

"Full of trouble."

Hawk moved forward as the dog eluded a well-intentioned guest.

The wedding had truly been disrupted now. Everyone had turned to watch the wily four-legged perpetrator of chaos.

The dog headed toward the back of the gathering, as if sensing that with another few passes, she'd be home free, dashing away from the assembled guests.

Hawk shoved back his chair as he moved into the aisle. He knew he had one shot at catching Victoria's renegade pooch.

He tensed and then dove forward as the furry and furious fuzzball tried to whiz by.

In mid-lunge, he heard gasps, and someone called out a bit of encouragement. And in the next moment, he'd caught the excited Finola with his outstretched arms before landing hard on the ground.

The dog relinquished the bouquet as she was tackled and started yapping again.

A few guests began clapping, and a man called out, "Well done."

Hawk held on firmly to the squirming animal as he straightened and then stood upright. He held Finola away from him.

Victoria rushed forward. "Here, Finola."

Pia snatched the battered bouquet, her expression one of disbelief mixed with dismay.

Hawk watched her, and then murmured, "Just remember, bad luck comes in threes."

She looked up at him, eyes wide. "Please tell me this is number three."

Before he could reassure Pia, Victoria reached to take Finola from him and then snuggled the dog close.

The bride started to laugh and some of the guests joined in. Others broke out into smiles.

Hawk watched Pia relax and smile herself. He could practically read her mind. *If the bride and everyone else could see the humor in the situation, then everything was going to be okay.*

"Who's been the naughty pooch, hmm?" Victoria said.

Hawk resisted rolling his eyes. *Perhaps he did have a preference for women who owned cats rather than dogs.*

With a wave of the arm, he acknowledged the scattered praise from the wedding guests and righted his fallen chair.

Victoria looked at him. "Thank you so much, Hawk. You saved the day."

Hawk glanced at Pia, a smile pulling at his lips. "Not at all. I'm glad I was able to be of service."

Pia lifted her eyebrows.

Victoria walked back up the aisle so the ceremony could resume, and Pia returned the bouquet to its position on the pedestal. Someone kept a firm hold on Finola.

Everything proceeded without a hitch after that. Much to Hawk's regret, though, Pia did not retake her seat next to him but chose to remain positioned near the front of the assembled guests. He couldn't blame her, though, in light of all the recent excitement.

Once the ceremony was over, however, he was able to approach her at the indoor reception, where he spotted her standing with her back to him near the open bar.

"Drink?" he said as he came up behind her.

She turned around at his query, looking as if she was

amused in spite of herself. "For some reason, I'm experiencing a sensation of déjà vu."

Hawk grinned. "I thought so." He chucked her under the chin. "You acquitted yourself splendidly today."

"With your help. Victoria seems to think you went above and beyond the call of duty."

"It was the least I could do," he demurred with a touch of self-mockery. "I was the one who got you involved with the crazy bride."

She smiled. "Only with the best of intentions."

Hawk felt momentarily dazzled by Pia's smile. She could light up a room with it, he thought. Give her a wand and she could sprinkle some glittering fairy dust, no problem.

He pushed aside the whimsical thought, and for Pia's benefit, he shook his head in resigned amusement. "A doggy attendant dressed up to match the bride? Who'd ever have thought it?"

"You'd be surprised," Pia returned. "I've even seen a pet pig march up the aisle."

"Well, Finola is no match for Mr. Darcy."

Pia laughed. "Mr. Darcy would agree with you, I'm sure."

They discussed the wedding at that point, with Pia remarking on how beautiful Victoria had looked, and Hawk commenting on some of the faces he recognized among the guests.

"This is a working party for me," Pia said eventually, as if to remind herself as much as him.

"I suppose you'll have to stay until the very end then?" he remarked.

She nodded. "I'll have to make sure everything is wrapped up."

Hawk looked through the reception room's paned windows and noted it was already dark.

"How are you getting back home?" he asked, guessing that she hadn't come in her own car because she'd had to borrow the services of his earlier.

She lifted a shoulder, and said simply, "I'll order a car service."

His eyes met hers. "I'll stick around then."

"I...i-it's not necessary."

"I know." He smiled. "Nevertheless, I'm at your disposal."

It wasn't until a few hours later that he was able to make good on his offer. He noted that Pia still managed to look as edible as dessert by the end of the evening, even though she also seemed drained.

They drove back to Manhattan mostly in silence, content to observe the darkened world whizzing by after a long day—and comfortable enough in each other's company not to make forced conversation.

When Hawk pulled up in front of Pia's building, however, he glanced over, only to notice that she had fallen asleep.

Her head was leaning back against the headrest, her lips parted.

He turned off the ignition and then stopped, taking a moment to study her face. For once, she looked unguarded.

Her blond hair had a fine, wispy quality, and he knew from experience that it was as soft as a baby's. Her eyebrows were delicately arched over eyes that he knew were large and expressive and a fascinating, changeable mix of amber hues.

Hawk let his gaze roam down to her lips. They held the sheen of a shimmery pink lipstick, but they needed no embellishment for their natural charm as far as he was concerned. He'd tasted them earlier in the day, because the temptation had been too great.

He debated for a moment, and then, unable to help himself,

leaned over, tilted her chin toward him with a light touch and pressed his lips to hers.

He rubbed his lips against hers, feeling the tingle of sensation, and then gently worked her lower lip with a small suck.

Dessert hadn't been nearly as good.

Pia's eyelashes fluttered. She opened her eyes and lifted her head.

Hawk pulled back, and then gave her a lopsided smile.

"Wh-what?"

"I was awakening Sleeping Beauty with a kiss," he responded in a low voice. "Isn't that the fairy-tale heroine that you are today?"

She blinked, coming further awake. "Unintentionally. This isn't a good idea."

He glanced past her and then back down again, keeping his expression innocent. "Did you prefer not to be awakened when we arrived at your apartment? Should I have driven straight on to my place instead?"

"Absolutely not," she said, though in a halfhearted tone.

He smiled for a moment before turning to open the driver-side door.

He reached her side of the car in time to help her alight, though she hesitated for a second before placing her hand in his.

By now, he was used to the sizzle of any physical contact between them.

"Good night, Your Grace," she said when she'd gotten out of his car, her eyes meeting his.

He let his lips drift upward. "Good night, Pia."

He watched as she made her way into her building, the doorman looking up from his television set to acknowledge her.

Only after she'd disappeared from view did he get back into his car.

As he pulled into traffic, Hawk acknowledged that he was pushing the boundaries with Pia. But, he told himself, he knew what the limits were.

Or so he hoped.

Seven

"*Ducal Gofer*. Gazillionaire bridal assistant, the Duke of Hawkshire…"

Pia gritted her teeth as she read Mrs. Jane Hollings's gossip column in *The New York Intelligencer*.

"What's wrong?" Belinda asked.

Pia had just sat down at a table in Contadini, where she, Belinda Wentworth and Tamara Langsford—née Kincaid— were having one of their Sunday brunch dates.

"Mrs. Hollings has written about me and Hawk in her gossip column," Pia said as she scrolled down the article on her smartphone. "Apparently she received notice that Hawk helped me handle some wedding escapades last night."

"That was fast," Belinda commented.

"Well, it's in her online column," Pia responded, looking up. "Her regular print one will appear in Monday's paper, where no doubt I will be able to savor the joy of having my name appear in print with—" her lips pulled down "—the Duke of Hawkshire's."

Belinda looked at Tamara. "Doesn't your husband own this paper? Can't you do something about this awful woman?"

Tamara cleared her throat. "I have news."

"You already told us, remember?" Belinda quipped. "We know you're knocked up, and Sawyer is the daddy."

"Old news." Tamara looked from Pia to Belinda. "The new news is that Sawyer and I plan to stay together."

"For the sake of the baby?" Belinda shook her head. "Honey…"

Tamara shook her head. "No, because we love each other."

Belinda stared at her blankly for a moment. Then she waved to a passing waiter. "Another Bloody Mary, please."

Pia knew this was a sore point for Belinda, since her friend still needed to get an annulment from the Marquess of Easterbridge.

"I suppose I should be addressing you both as *My Lady,*" Pia mused. "Sawyer is an earl, making Tamara a countess, and since Colin is a marquess, you're entitled to be called—"

"Don't you dare," Belinda retorted. "I'm planning to shed the title as soon as possible."

Pia sighed. "Oh, well."

Belinda turned to Tamara. "I can't believe you're abandoning our trio of girlfriends for the aristocratic cadre."

"I'm not. It's just…"

"What?" Belinda asked, her expression sardonic. "You moved in with Sawyer and made a marriage of convenience. And then—" she snapped her fingers "—next thing you know, you're pregnant with his child and declaring yourself in love."

Tamara smiled and shrugged. "It's the most exciting thing that's ever happened to me," she admitted. "I wasn't looking to fall in love, and if you'd asked me months ago, I'd have said Sawyer was the last man…"

Tamara got a faraway look as her words drifted off. "I realized Sawyer was the one I wanted all along," she eventually continued. "And the best part is he feels the same way about me."

Belinda accepted the Bloody Mary that the waiter was about to set down in front of her, and took a healthy swig. "Well, I'm happy for you, Tam. One of us deserves to find happiness."

Tamara gave a faint smile. "Thanks. I know you and Pia don't like Sawyer's friends—"

"You mean my husband?" Belinda asked archly.

"You mean Hawk?" Pia said at the same time.

"—but Sawyer and I are hoping you all will make nice enough to be in the same room together. In fact, we're hoping to have all of you over next Saturday night for a small postwedding celebration."

"A we're-staying-married party?" Belinda queried.

"Sort of," Tamara acknowledged before looking across at Pia, who'd taken the seat to Belinda's right. "Please come. You love anything having to do with weddings."

Pia sighed again. She did. And she hated to disappoint Tamara, though it wasn't wise for her to spend too much time in Hawk's company.

"How are you getting along with Hawk these days, Pia?" Tamara asked suddenly, as if reading her mind. "I know you're planning his sister's wedding. And you just noted that Mrs. Hollings is gossiping about how he helped you last night."

Pia hesitated. How much should she reveal? Certainly not the stolen kisses—and the fact that she'd enjoyed them.

He'd said he was trying to make amends. And so far, she'd let him. *More than let him.*

The kisses came back to her. The tingle of excitement, the remembered feeling of delicious passion—just like the first time, and just like in her dreams—and the sensation of melding with a kindred spirit.

Pia shook her head slightly as if to clear it. *No.*

She was playing with fire, and she'd be foolhardy to go down that road again.

And yet...

She'd felt an acute sadness for Hawk when she'd discovered what had precipitated his abrupt departure from her apartment after they'd slept together. Her parents were alive and well back in Pennsylvania, and while she didn't have any siblings, she imagined that Hawk had been understandably devastated by the unexpected loss of his brother.

None of this is intended as an excuse.

Hawk had still acted toward her as if he felt he was at fault and was feeling guilty. Of course, his brother's untimely death didn't explain why he hadn't sought her out after their night together. Had the abrupt severing of ties made it easy for him to forget her? The thought hurt. And yet what other explanation could there be? She hadn't meant enough to him.

And yet...

She knew even if she softened toward him, let their explosive chemistry play out to its natural conclusion, this time she would no longer be the naive virgin who was new in town. She could show Hawk that she could play in more sophisticated circles, too, these days.

He was flirting with her, and she could enjoy it and not become besotted.

Why couldn't she be one of those women who enjoyed a fling or a casual hookup? She'd already had a one-night stand. *With him.*

These thoughts and more flitted through her mind.

Pia became aware of Belinda and Tamara staring at her.

She cleared her throat. "Hawk has been...helpful," she hedged, and then shrugged. "I—I suppose I'm feeling ambivalent at best."

"Ambivalent?" Belinda questioned, and then rolled her eyes. "Isn't that one step away from infatuated these days? Pia, please tell me you're not falling for the guy again."

"Of course not!"

"Because you have a soft heart, and I'd hate to—"

"D-don't worry. Once burned, twice shy." She shrugged. "But I am planning his sister's wedding, and I do need to be on cordial terms with him."

"Great," Tamara commented. "I'm so glad you won't have any trouble being in Hawk's company next weekend."

Belinda frowned. "It's not Hawk I'm worried about."

Pia refused to admit that Hawk *was* the one *she* was worried about.

Hawk took another sip of his wine and his senses came fully alert.

Pia.

He spotted her immediately when she came into the parlor of the Earl and Countess of Melton's Upper East Side town house. But it was as if he'd been able to sense her presence even before seeing her.

She looked spectacular. Her high-waist sheath dress with its black bodice and white skirt flattered her curves, making her seem taller than she was and showing off her great legs in black patent peep-toe pumps.

He glimpsed the deep pink color of the nail polish on her toes, and his gut tightened.

Heaven help him, but she packed a wallop in a small package. It was almost as if she'd been sent to entice him—to test his best resolutions.

He started toward her, but was suddenly stopped by a staying hand on his arm.

He turned his head to look inquiringly at Colin, Marquess of Easterbridge.

Colin gave him a careless smile. "Careful there. Your lady-killer ways are showing."

Hawk let the side of his mouth quirk up. "The opposite is more likely the case. She looks harmless but—"

Colin laughed shortly. "They all do."

Hawk had no doubt the marquess was also referencing his own wife, Belinda Wentworth, who legally remained the Marchioness of Easterbridge. Hawk was curious about the exact state of affairs between Colin and Belinda these days, but he didn't want to pry. Colin was an enigma even to his friends at times.

"I have it covered," Hawk responded. "I'm proceeding only with the best reconnaissance."

Colin gave another knowing laugh. "I'll wager you are."

Hawk shrugged, and then started toward Pia again, leaving Colin standing where he was.

So what if the look he'd given Pia made it clear that he found her desirable, and everyone knew it?

Pia was looking at *him* expectantly right now, though there was also puzzlement in her eyes—as if she wondered about his brief exchange with Colin.

"I won't offer you a drink," he quipped as he reached her. "You look fabulous, by the way."

There was no *by the way* about it, he thought. Everything else was tangential.

Pia flushed. "Th-thank you. I wouldn't mind a glass of wine."

He snagged a couple from a waiter who happened by, and handed one to her.

"Cheers," he said as he clinked his glass to hers. "How is the wedding planning going? I understand from my sister that she's been to your apartment twice this week."

Pia took a sip of her drink. "Yes, we were discussing invitations and décor. Fortunately, she already had a dress picked out." She smiled as if sharing a joke. "Everything with this wedding is going smoothly, so far."

"I've only been to your apartment once. Can I express envy?"

Pia raised her eyebrows for a moment, and then laughed. She tapped him on the wrist. "Only if you play your cards right."

Hawk hesitated. If he'd heard her correctly, she'd just met his flirtation with a bit of her own. He was used to banter between them, but it wasn't usually so…receptive.

"How is Mr. Darcy?" he tried, testing. "Perhaps he's in need of a male role model?"

"If he is, would you be one?"

Ah. "I am more than willing to try."

Pia gave an exaggerated sigh. "Are you ever serious?"

In response, he banked his amusement.

"Would it matter if I said yes?"

Though he could lapse into well-practiced flirtation—he remembered his old self well—he felt the weight of his responsibilities too much these days to be anything other than what was expected of him. A duke.

Pia searched his eyes, and he held her amber ones solemnly.

"That comment was rather unfair of me," she said. "I've seen how you feel a responsibility to your sister as the head of the family. A-and you've certainly helped me."

"Lucy has been talking?" he queried, not answering her directly.

She nodded.

"Burnishing my image, that's my girl."

Over Pia's shoulder, Hawk glimpsed Colin approach Belinda before Pia's friend turned on her heel and stalked toward the door. Colin followed at a more leisurely pace, drink in hand.

Realizing that she no longer held his attention, Pia turned

in the direction of his gaze. "Oh, dear," she said in a low voice as she swung back to face him. "Was that a confrontation I just missed?"

Hawk looked down at her. "A near-miss. Belinda walked away before Easterbridge could approach her."

"In contrast to you and me."

He shot her a surprised look, and then gave her a game smile. "Some of us are lucky."

Pia sighed. "Easterbridge should give Belinda the annulment that she's looking for, and let her move on with her life. Instead, he seems to enjoy tormenting her."

"My friends are not unlikable, despite what you may believe."

"In a way, it's hard to believe that you and Easterbridge are friends. He can't get unmarried, while you—"

Hawk quirked a brow. "Yes?"

"—have never been married," she finished lamely.

He could tell from the look in Pia's eyes, however, that she had intended to label him a commitment-shy player. The fact that she hadn't said something, at least.

Had Lucy's words had a salutary effect on Pia's opinion of him? There was only one way to find out.

Hawk took a sip of his wine. "Let's turn back to a more soothing subject for my ego. Lucy has been singing my praises."

A small smile rose to Pia's lips, and she nodded. "Lucy mentioned that you've been working nonstop these past three years as you've moved into your role as duke, learned the running of the estates and started Sunhill Investments."

"Are you surprised?"

Pia hesitated, and then shook her head. "No. You've acted… differently than you did three years ago." She paused. "It must have been very hard for you after your father and brother died."

He didn't recollect stories about his father and his brother every day anymore—not like three years ago—but their joint passing had set his life on a new trajectory. "William and I were two years apart. We grew up as friends and playmates as well as brothers, though I always knew I got a free pass as the younger son while William had his life and responsibilities mapped out for him."

It was more personal information than he was accustomed to divulging.

Pia didn't look as if she was sitting in judgment, however. "And then one day the free pass disappeared…"

He nodded. "As fate would have it."

"You had a reputation as a player," she stated without inflection. "The stories—"

"Old news, but reports will hang around the internet forever." His mouth twisted. "I do have two jobs that often take up more time than one person can handle, believe it or not. I do need to be serious for those."

"I've hardly had an opportunity to see it," she protested.

He'd meant to tweak her nose about her earlier query about his lack of seriousness, and he could tell she understood it.

"Maybe you just bring out the devilish side of me." He tilted his head. "Perhaps with you, I can relax and tease."

She flushed. "I'm such an easy target."

"You hold your own," he offered, taken in by her blush.

She moistened her lips, and he watched longingly.

"Would you like to see a more intense and focused side of me?" he asked, suddenly going with an idea. "I'm going rock climbing at a gym in Brooklyn tomorrow. The gym keeps me in shape for the real thing."

Pia's eyes glinted. "Who ever heard of a duke rock climbing?"

He assumed a suitable hauteur. "I'm a modern-day duke. This is an outlet for all those go-forth-and-conquer genes that my ancestors bequeathed to me."

"All right."

Accepting her response, he didn't add that rock climbing was also a good pressure-release valve.

Because right now, he was feeling an ungodly urge to conquer and possess *her*.

Eight

He had his hands all over her.

At least that's how it felt to Pia.

Between teaching her how to use the equipment and instructing her on how to place her feet on the climbing wall, it felt as if Hawk had covered her body even more thoroughly this morning at the gym than he might have in bed.

Downing a flavored-water drink, her heart thumping with spent energy, and sweat soaking her sports bra and biker shorts, she eyed Hawk and tried not to think of jumping him.

She was petite and a featherweight, so she doubted that even if she launched herself at him, he'd do more than stagger a step—if that.

He looked all primal male standing in the middle of the cavernous gym in his own sweat-dampened shirt and shorts, his lean, muscular frame exposed to her avid gaze. It was a sign of how physically fit he was, however, that *he'd* only perspired a little.

Still, she could smell the sweat—and, yes, she could swear, even the male hormones on him—and her body reacted in response. She willed her nipples not to become more pronounced. With any luck, he'd think it was all due to a blast of cool air hitting her damp skin, anyway.

Finishing off a swallow of water, Hawk eyed her speculatively as he capped his bottle. "You're the first woman who has indulged my rock-climbing hobby. You're the only one who, astonishingly, agreed to come along for the ride."

"So I was hoodwinked by you?" she teased, though inside she felt a thrill at his admission.

"You did well," he said, sidestepping the question. "You made it to the top of the wall and down." His eyes gleamed with respect and admiration. "More than once, in fact. Congratulations."

"Thank you."

She didn't know why it should matter that she'd proven herself at one of Hawk's pastimes—aside from fishing and horseback riding—but it did.

Even though it was a Sunday morning, several other patrons moved around them in the open gym.

Pia realized that she was tagging along on one of Hawk's regular workouts, except it hadn't been the typical gym that they'd gone to when he'd picked her up at her apartment in his car this morning. She did not have a wedding to attend to this weekend, so she'd easily been able to rise early herself.

She capped her drink bottle. She realized that she'd slaked her thirst—for water, anyway.

"Have you ever encountered one of your namesakes on any of your rock-climbing adventures?" she asked to make conversation.

She tried to distract herself from what he looked like in his clingy gym clothes.

He looked amused. "Have I met a hawk?" He shook his head. "Only once. I don't think the bird was impressed."

She wet her lips. "Did you become known as Hawk upon assuming the title?"

He nodded. "My father was known as Hawkshire, in the customary way of addressing peers by their titles rather than their given names. It felt right to distinguish myself in some way when I assumed the title. But in the end, I didn't have a say in the matter. Easterbridge and Melton began calling me Hawk, and it caught on."

She contemplated him. "It suits you."

He rubbed the bridge of his nose, looking further amused. "You mean this?"

"How did you break your nose?" she asked, glad that he didn't look insulted.

"Ah…" He smiled, but then hesitated. "At the risk of highlighting my former raffish ways, I'll admit to getting into a barroom brawl during my university days."

"Through no fault of your own, of course."

"Naturally," he deadpanned, dimpling. "And all participants have been barred from speaking further about the matter."

"I'll bet Easterbridge or Melton would know."

Hawk laughed. "You're at liberty to attempt to unearth the information."

"Maybe I'll try," she responded lightly.

He glanced down at himself and then at her, his gaze seeming to linger on all her softest places. "In the meantime, why don't we get ourselves ready and get out of here?"

She nodded. "Okay."

"Don't you have an appointment to meet with Lucy this afternoon at the house?"

She nodded again. "Lucy's understudy is filling in for her for today's performances."

"Then why don't you come straight back with me?" he offered. "The house will be a more comfortable place for you to shower and change than the gym. We could have something to eat and kill some time before you need to take your meeting with Lucy."

Pia hesitated. Shower and change at his residence? *No, no, no.* She thought of her gym bag in her locker. In the ladies' room, she'd be safe and surrounded by other members of the female tribe—not by a descendant of conquerors.

Hawk smiled. "I promise I won't bite. There are a couple of guest bedrooms with en suite bathrooms where you'll feel comfortable. You choose."

Pia blushed because it seemed he'd read her mind.

But, then again, what could it hurt to accede to his suggestion? Lucy would most likely be at home or there soon, and then there would be the presence of the household help.

Except when they got back to Hawk's house, Pia discovered that Lucy was not home and not expected back until shortly before her afternoon appointment with Pia. The staff, typically discreet, was nowhere to be seen.

Nevertheless, she chose a guest bedroom with cheery yellow-and-blue-chintz upholstery and a white canopy bed. She showered in the adjoining marble bath, and then wrapped herself in a plush blue towel.

The house was clearly appointed with luxury throughout, she realized. Before now, she'd only been in Hawk's home to talk with Lucy, and she'd never been on the upper levels.

As she came out of the bathroom, Pia eyed the bed. It was tempting to allow herself to sink onto it and revel in its comfort. The mattress and the counterpane seemed soft and thick. In fact, the whole bedroom was decorated in a way she'd have aspired to in her apartment if she'd had the money. Instead, she'd contented herself with the budget version of many items.

Turning away from temptation, she dressed, pulling on an emerald top with a square neckline edged with red ribbon. She paired it with a full taupe skirt, wide black patent belt, black leggings and gold ballerina flats.

Today, the weather was a little cooler, the breeze having a little nip, so she'd pulled some of her fall attire from her wardrobe while packing her gym bag.

When she was done getting ready, she wandered out of the bedroom and down the hall. Stopping before the door of the bedroom that Hawk had pointed out to her as his, she hesitated just a moment before knocking.

When Hawk opened his door, however, she found herself swallowing and wetting her lips.

He wore a crisp white shirt and black pants, and his hair was still damp from his shower. He exuded a virile magnetism.

Why must he look so effortlessly but devastatingly attractive?

And then he looked at *her,* his eyes making a quick but thorough perusal.

He smiled, slow and sexy, and Pia felt her heart thump.

"A gorgeous woman knocking on my door. Under other circumstances, my next move would have been to invite you in and—" he winked "—allow my licentious nature free rein."

She heated. "I—I didn't want to wander around your house by myself, and I didn't know where we'd be having lunch." She decided to try to lighten the moment. "Heaven forbid someone spotted me and thought I was snooping."

His smile widened. "Which fairy-tale heroine goes around snooping? I can't recall."

"No one," she protested. "A-and I—I don't believe in fairy tales."

He took her hand. "Great, then we'll just have to make up our own story."

He stepped aside and tugged her into his room.

As Pia glanced around, Hawk made a sweeping motion with his arm.

"This is my bedroom." He shot her a devilish smile. "In case you were wondering what it looked like. Or should I say, in this tale, the heroine *wants to know* what it looks like."

And she wanted him to want her.

The thought flashed through her mind, and she couldn't deny its truth.

She made a visual sweep of the room. "V-very nice."

Dark, rich furniture contrasted with stripe and damask upholstery in varying shades of cream and green.

A four-poster bed was dominated by a scrolled wooden headboard.

She parted and then wet her lips.

Her eyes connected with Hawk's, and she realized that he'd caught every reaction.

She wanted to say something, and then stopped.

"I hate my speech impediment," she blurted inanely.

He gave a lopsided smile. "I love your verbal quirk." He leaned close, a twinkle in his eye. "It tells me just how much I'm affecting you."

She felt flustered because he was affecting her right now. "Mmm…y-you p-promised you wouldn't bite."

"Little Red Riding Hood and the Big, Bad Wolf?" he queried as he moved closer. "Okay, I can work with that story line."

Despite herself, she laughed. "You're incorrigible."

He reached out and caressed her arm. "I promised I wouldn't bite, but that leaves much unbargained territory."

"I am not Little Red Riding Hood."

"Of course," he agreed soothingly. "Not into role-play?"

She gave a helpless laugh.

He ducked his head and brushed his lips across hers.

He made to pull back almost immediately, but then his lips lowered to hers again—as if Hawk couldn't help himself—and this time the kiss lingered.

Hawk's arms came around her, and she slid her own up to his neck. They pressed close, hard planes meeting soft curves and fitting together without gap, despite their difference in height.

He tasted minty and fresh, and as his tongue invaded her mouth, she made a sound deep in her throat and met him eagerly.

The kiss was intense, but finally slowed.

"Pia," Hawk muttered against her mouth. "It's been too long. How could I ever forget?"

She didn't want him ever to forget. She wanted him to remember her in the way he'd similarly always be with her.

She'd always remember him. *Her first lover.*

Suddenly Hawk bent and hooked his arm under her knees, and laid her on the bed. He came down beside her and took her in his arms again.

"Pia." He brushed the hair away from her face. "You remind me of a nymph or a fairy."

"I suppose it doesn't help that I'm wearing ballerina flats today."

He gave a short laugh. "Even when you're not in flats, you're petite." He brushed her hair so that it fanned out over the coverlet. "I've never seen a wood nymph climb a rock wall before."

She wrinkled her nose at his words as his delicious weight pressed her into the mattress. "I can just imagine what I looked like from the ground."

"I had trouble stopping myself from reaching out and doing this," he said, caressing her leg.

"Oh."

Hawk shifted, his knee wedging between her legs as he leaned over her. He kissed her then, sipping at her lips and lazily tracing their outline with his tongue.

"L-lucy will come home," Pia breathed against his mouth.

"Not for a long time," he whispered back.

Pia felt his arousal press against her, evidence of his growing need. Mirroring his response, her nipples felt tight, and a moist heat had gathered between her thighs.

She shifted. "Why did I bother getting dressed?"

Her remark elicited a low chuckle from him, and she felt it reverberate through his chest.

He placed a moist kiss near her ear. "Don't worry. We can remedy the situation."

True to his word, he made quick work of her shoes and leggings, and then settled himself between her legs.

She felt his warm breath on her thigh, and her delicate skin was stroked by the slight abrasiveness of his jaw.

He squeezed her calf as his lips grazed her thigh. He let his lips trail down first one leg and then the other.

Pia quivered in response.

In the next moment, she moaned as he sucked on her tender flesh. She couldn't help herself, but it seemed to excite him to hear how he was making her feel.

Her hands tangled in his hair, and she urged him upward for an urgent kiss. She met him halfway, sitting up, and they kissed, his hands wandering her back urgently.

She was crazy to think she could be unforgettable to a man of his experience. She was loony to think she could match his level of sophistication in seduction.

But then he obliged her with a groan deep in his throat. "Ah, Pia…what you do to me."

She rubbed his arousal. "I can tell."

He grew in a sharp breath. "You're not as shy as I remembered."

She hoped not.

Since he'd left her, she'd made a point of studying romantic movies, reading a book or two and renting some videos—all in an attempt to overcome some of her naiveté and inexperience. She'd thought she'd never have fallen for Hawk's practiced skills if she'd been more knowledgeable. And at the same time, irrationally, she'd started to believe that Hawk wouldn't have left her if she'd been more of a seductress.

Still, she didn't think now was the time to mention to him that she'd been educating herself.

Instead, she tilted her head, and asked innocently, "You don't want me to be...uninhibited?"

"Of course I'd love it."

She gave him a smile.

"How am I going to get you out of these clothes?" he mused, his eyes sweeping over her.

She straightened, and then slid off the bed and turned to face him. "You won't have to. I-I'm going to strip for you."

He smiled, slow and sexy, doing funny things to her insides.

The room was cool and shadowed, the shades apparently still drawn from when he was dressing and undressing.

Pia pulled her top over her head and tossed it on a dresser.

Catching Hawk's hot gaze, she teased him by tracing the edges of her lacy pink bra with her fingertips.

Hawk continued avidly watching her with hooded eyes.

Pia wet her lips, running the tip of her tongue over the plump and swollen formation of her mouth.

She still felt the imprint of Hawk's kisses there. And judging from the look of him, Hawk was on a tight leash, stopping himself from giving her more and then some.

"This is going to be the shortest strip on record," he murmured thickly. "Need some help there?"

She knew her nipples were outlined against the nylon fabric of her bra, the coolness of the room adding to her arousal. Her breasts were a bit oversized for her frame, giving her the appearance of a busty fairy. However, since high school, she hadn't caught a guy eyeing them as lustily as Hawk was.

She shivered, and Hawk crooked his finger at her.

Her stomach did a somersault.

She came to him, and he caught her, leaning back to lie down on the bed as she straddled him.

Mouth met mouth in a voracious kiss. Then he was feasting

on her breasts, and she threw back her head and luxuriated in the sensation.

"Hawk."

He unclasped her bra and peeled away the offending barrier, his mouth barely leaving her in the process. He suckled her, his hands bunching her breasts together for his greedy lips.

Pia felt sweet and piercing-hot sensations shoot through her. In response, she rubbed against him.

Hawk lifted his mouth from her breast and sat up so they were face-to-face. "If we don't slow down," he muttered thickly, his mouth close to hers, "this is going to be over in two minutes."

"Th-three y-years is a long time to wait."

"Too long."

With one hand, she opened the first button of his shirt, and then the next and the next. All the while, she was aware of the rasp of his breath as her gaze focused on the strong column of his throat.

She finally undid his cuffs and tugged at his shirt.

He obliged her by sitting up and shrugging out of his white shirt and the undershirt below.

He quirked his lips. "Now what?"

"D-do you have a blindfold for yourself?"

He laughed helplessly.

"You're only half-naked," she protested.

"It's a situation I'm more than happy to rectify."

She moved aside, and he got off the bed.

But before he could make a further move, she stopped him, laying a hand on his arm.

"Let me."

Getting up herself, she worked slowly but surely, her hands brushing his arousal and causing his breathing to deepen.

She slid his belt free of its loops and then lowered his zipper.

He helped her then, and the room sounded with the thud of his shoes and the slither of his pants and boxers.

Pia caressed his arousal freely before bending and kneeling before him.

Hawk groaned. "Pia, Pia...ah, sweet."

Pia was lost in the experience of making love in a way she never had before. She felt the tension in Hawk's muscles and the throbbing heat of his flesh. And when she gave him the most intimate kiss she could imagine, he stiffened and groaned again, gripping the bedside table.

"Pia," Hawk said, his voice heavy and thick with arousal. "You've definitely...changed."

She'd had time over the past three years to replay the night she'd lost her innocence to Hawk. She'd had time to imagine different scenarios. She'd had time to see herself as the seductress instead of the one being seduced.

And now, unexpectedly, she had a chance to realize some of those fantasies. *With him.* Because he'd always been the lover whom she'd imagined.

She focused on giving pleasure and soaking in the sounds of how much Hawk was enjoying her ministrations.

She wanted to make him lose control.

Moments ticked by, and then, on an oath, Hawk disengaged her, pulling her up for a rough kiss.

"I'm not going to ask where you learned that," he said darkly.

If only he knew, Pia thought.

She thrilled at the tacit admission that she'd given him unexpected pleasure. She warmed to the tinge of jealousy in his voice.

"T-take me," she said, her request a plea and a demand. "H-Hawk, p-please."

He swept her up into his arms and laid her on the bed again. He rid her of her belted skirt, her last piece of clothing and of protection from his avid gaze.

He leaned over her and caressed her body. "You're so beautiful, you make me ache."

Pia felt her heart squeeze.

"Are you using any protection?" he asked.

She shook her head. "No."

He opened a nearby nightstand drawer and removed a packet.

"I don't think I can be near you without being prepared," he said with self-deprecation.

She gave a small smile. "S-sort of like leaving the house without your BlackBerry?"

He chuckled. "Sort of. But you make me lose my mind, whether I like it or not."

He sheathed himself, and Pia reached her arms up to him.

She wanted him to lose control right now. The need to be joined to him was overwhelming. She wanted to experience falling over the edge again with him into paradise. It had been so long…

Hawk settled his weight on her. "Ah, Pia, let me in…"

He entered her, and they both closed their eyes, savoring the sweet sensation of their joining.

Hawk started to move, and a delicious friction began to build in Pia.

They kissed and moaned, and he bit down gently on the tender skin at the side of her throat, while she let her hands roam over his hard muscles, urging him onward.

Pia convulsed gently, once and then twice.

"That's right," Hawk muttered. "Come for me, Pia. Come again."

He whispered sweet encouragement.

Pia felt herself tremble, her body on the cusp of deliverance. She tightened around Hawk, and her hands fell from his back to grasp the coverlet.

He was relentless in pursuit of her pleasure. "Pia," he breathed in her ear. "Sweetheart, tell me."

"H-Hawk, p-please, y-yes."

The sound of how much he affected her was his undoing.

Hawk groaned and stilled just as her body began to shake. He spilled himself inside her, wondrously joining her powerful climax with one of his own.

Pia cried out with her release, and Hawk clasped her to him, his skin hot and damp.

Their hearts racing, they came back down to earth—or some version of it.

This, she thought, was what dreams were made of.

Nine

In the normal course of things, lunch with Colin, Marquess of Easterbridge, and Sawyer Langsford, Earl of Melton, in the dining room of the historic Sherry-Netherland Hotel should have been a tame and relaxing affair.

Hawk knew better.

Lately, notoriety had come nipping at the heels of his trio of friends.

Colin looked up quizzically from his BlackBerry. "Well, Melton, it seems Mrs. Hollings has done it again."

Sawyer nodded at a waiter who then proceeded to fill his wineglass, and took his time addressing Colin. "What, pray tell, has she deemed worthy of acid ink this time?"

"The topic is us…again," Colin said, his tone bland. "Or, more exactly, the subject is Hawkshire."

"How very fair of you, Melton," Hawk commented dryly, "to include us in the *Intelligencer's* gossip column."

Sawyer's lips quirked. "So what does our Mrs. Hollings have to say today?"

"Apparently Hawkshire has a second career as a wedding planner's apprentice."

Sawyer raised his eyebrows and swiveled his head to look at Hawk, his expression droll. "And you kept this tidbit from us? How could you?"

Damnation. Hawk knew he was in for a ribbing from his two friends. Still, it was worth mounting a defense, however feeble. "My sister is getting married."

"'We've heard,'" Colin said, quoting the text from his BlackBerry, "'that a certain very wealthy duke has been keeping company with a lovely wedding planner. Could it be that wedding bells are in the air?'"

"Charming, our Mrs. Hollings," Sawyer said.

"A veritable fount of useful information."

Hawk remained steadfastly mum, refusing to add his two cents to his friends' comments.

Sawyer frowned. "How is your mother these days, Hawk? The last time I had the opportunity to be in her charming company, she talked of finding you a bride. In fact, I believe one name in particular crossed her lips."

"Michelene Ward-Fombley," Hawk said succinctly.

Sawyer nodded. "Ah, yes, that sounds—" he paused to give Hawk a shrewd look "—exactly right… A suitable choice."

Of course, Sawyer and Colin would have a passing acquaintance with Michelene, Hawk thought. She was from their aristocratic social circle. Her grandfather was a viscount, not someone from a small town in Pennsylvania…

He and Michelene had dated a few times, back when he was still trying to sort out what his role as the new duke should be. He'd gingerly tested the waters by stepping into William's shoes with one of the leading candidates to be a future duchess. But then his work with Sunhill Investments had consumed him, and still grieving, he'd allowed himself to stop calling Michelene. It had been easy to do, since she hadn't awakened any strong emotion in him. But then, in the past year, the idea of Michelene as the Duchess of Hawkshire had gained renewed life, thanks to his mother's prodding.

"What game are you playing, Hawk?" Sawyer asked, going straight to the point.

Hawk kept his expression steady. Ever since Sawyer's marriage of convenience to Tamara had turned into a real one, he'd been protective of her and her girlfriends, Pia and Belinda.

Pia.

Damn it, he was not going to discuss Pia with Melton or Easterbridge.

Yesterday had been the most passionate experience of his life—for the second time. Inexplicably, he felt a visceral connection to Pia. Maybe that explained why he'd never forgotten her...

She'd been a virgin, but if last night was anything to judge by, she'd learned a lot in the past three years.

He acknowledged as much with a punch to the gut. He'd been unprepared for the Pia of yesterday afternoon. She'd caught him by surprise—again. He'd intended to be the seducer, and instead had been seduced.

Yet...had he really intended to seduce her again? Despite all his noble intentions?

Certainly, by the time she'd entered his bedroom, his mind had turned toward kissing her and more. But the idea had been gaining steam well before then. Without a doubt, while she'd been giving him a tantalizing view of her luscious posterior all morning. And maybe even before then...when she'd been running across the grass toward him at the New York Botanical Garden, or when...

He wanted her. All he'd been able to think about for the past twenty-four hours was getting Pia in bed again. And now that they'd crossed the threshold to being lovers again, he admitted he also didn't want to turn back. He wanted to remain lovers—unlike the first time three years ago—even if his relatively newfound principles were in jeopardy as a result!

They'd been forced to end their afternoon tryst yesterday when Lucy had arrived home. Otherwise, Hawk was sure that he and Pia would have spent all day in bed.

Instead, Pia had descended the stairs as if nothing untoward had happened—such as Lucy's wedding planner having completely undone her brother—and had met with Lucy as if she'd arrived at the house only a little early and had been awaiting her.

Why was it so upsetting that their lovemaking left her so unaffected? He couldn't fall into a too serious entanglement with her—not with all his responsibilities to his title.

Hawk noted belatedly that Sawyer was waiting for an answer, and even Colin looked intent.

"There's no game," he said, choosing his words with care.

Blast it, even *he* didn't know what to make of his relationship with Pia. Not anymore. He had no compass.

Sawyer looked dubious. "Then you're not practically eng—"

"There is no game," he repeated.

Sawyer eyed him, his expression thoughtful. "You might want to make sure Pia doesn't get hurt, either."

Right. If anything, Hawk thought, *he* was the one in danger here.

Pia felt a quiver of anticipation when her doorman rang and announced that Hawk was downstairs.

"Tell him to come up," she said before replacing her receiver and turning away from the phone.

She hugged herself and glanced at Mr. Darcy, who was eyeing her like a friend resigned to watching her make the same mistake twice.

She could sense the feline's disapproval—almost read his thoughts, if that were possible.

Wickham. Him again. Have we learned nothing?

"Oh, don't look at me that way," Pia said. "His name is not Wickham, as you well know. And I'm sure he has a very good reason for being here."

Right. And a cat has nine lives. I wish.

"You're way too cynical for a feline. Why did I adopt you from the shelter?"

You know why. I'm the antidote to your trusting romantic nature.

I'm not as naive as I once was, Pia responded in her head.

Mr. Darcy turned and padded toward his basket, set against one wall of her living room space. He stepped in, made himself comfortable and closed his eyes.

Pia stood there and then blushed as she remembered her afternoon idyll with Hawk on Sunday.

It was shocking how easily she lost her inhibitions with him. She'd forgotten herself in the moment. But he'd seemed equally affected.

At least she hoped so.

She still couldn't quite believe her daring—or foolhardiness—in trying to play in Hawk's league of seduction. She'd met him and upped the ante. And though she hadn't been able to admit it to herself, perhaps she'd set out to prove that she could bind him, unlike their first time.

Careful, careful. She couldn't and wouldn't risk her heart again. She was beyond being the naive virgin who believed in fairy tales. Instead, she'd take what she wanted from Hawk for her pleasure and be prepared to say goodbye with no regrets when the time came.

She looked at the clock. It was just after five. He must have come directly uptown to see her after the close of the New York financial markets.

She hadn't seen him since they'd wound up in bed together, but that was about to change.

Hawk stepped out of the elevator and immediately spotted Pia at her door—waiting for him.

"H-Hawk," Pia said, her voice a touch breathless.

She was dressed in a casual, cinched blue dress, her hair loose and with just a touch of shine to her lips.

She looked good enough to eat.

Without hesitation, he strode to her, wrapped his arms around her and gave her a bone-melting kiss.

When he finally lifted his head, he searched her gaze. "Blast it, I get so aroused when I hear you stutter."

She blushed. "I don't know why. Th-that has to be one of the most unusual compliments a woman has ever received."

He kissed her nose. "Do you know it's the most erotic thing in bed when your adorable speech tick is on full display?"

"How embarrassing."

"How perfect."

"*Oh.*"

Over Pia's shoulder, Hawk noticed Mr. Darcy lift his head from his cushioned basket and eye him.

Hawk got the sense that the pet's opinion of him had soured since the first time he'd been in Pia's apartment. Perhaps the cat had figured out who he was: The Duke Formerly Known as Mr. Wickham. Or rather, Mr. Fielding—wicked and wrong—as the case might be.

He held the feline's stare, giving the cat a stern but reassuring look, until Mr. Darcy lowered his head, closed his eyes and went back to his nap.

"Is something wrong?" Pia asked, stepping back and letting him into the apartment.

He followed her in and waited while she shut the door behind him.

Then he slid an arm around her waist and pulled her close. "Nothing is wrong except that since Sunday I've been desperate to see you."

He'd left work early to come here, hoping his appearance would be a welcome surprise. And judging from Pia's reaction, he'd bet right.

Pia slid her arms around his neck. "Oh?"

"I had a storm of work this week, and by the time I flew back from Chicago last night, I knew phone calls were no longer enough to sustain me."

"Mmm—really?"

He nuzzled her ear. "Nothing but your presence would do."

"You know, Your Grace," she responded playfully, "this is rather irregular. A client could arrive at any moment, or the phone could ring. We're on work hours."

He lifted his head to look into her eyes. "Are you expecting anyone this late in the day?"

"No," she admitted.

"Then there's no problem, as far as I see."

"There *is* a problem," she teased. "This has all the trappings of the lord of the manor cornering the backstairs maid."

"Because you're on my payroll?" he murmured, grazing her temple with his lips.

She nodded. "Exactly right. W-we had sexual relations in your bedroom right before I was to meet with your sister about wedding plans."

He almost laughed at her mock prudish tone even as *every* part of him was coming to stimulating arousal. He was finding this interchange with Pia more erotic than any of the more blatant attempts at seduction he'd been the recipient of in the past. It appeared that, after all, Pia might be skilled at role-play…

"Perhaps I should ask directly," he said, playing along. "Will you nevertheless oblige me?"

Pia tilted her head, pretending to consider. "Mmm…"

Not waiting for a response, he stroked her leg, and then let his hand wander under the hem of her dress until it connected with her hip. Sliding her panties to one side, he caressed her intimately.

He watched as her eyes clouded with desire.

"I want to know every inch of you," he murmured. "I want to taste your flavor and learn your scent."

Pia's eyelids drooped, and she gripped his arm hard.

"Pia?" he murmured when she still hadn't said anything.

He scanned her face and watched her eyelashes flutter against her pale skin.

She wet her lips. "Oh, y-yes. I-I'll oblige you."

They were both so turned on, they could hardly speak.

"This is the most erotic exchange I've ever had," she said as if she'd read his mind.

He had to have her. He kissed her, and then, removing his hand from under her dress, he wrapped his arms around her and lifted her off her feet.

He headed with her toward the bedroom.

"Are we destined to make love in the afternoon?" she asked.

He glanced down at her, a smile hovering at his lips. "Anytime becomes you, princess."

He stepped into her bedroom and deposited her on the bed, on top of her feminine white coverlet.

Straightening, he took a moment to let his eyes travel over her.

She looked up at him with desire. Her golden hair was spread out over the cover, and her lips were pink and wet from his kisses.

She was beautiful.

Pia parted her lips. "Oh, H-Hawk."

He closed his eyes and drew in a deep breath.

When he opened them again, he said with helpless amusement, "Don't say another word. I may go up in flames."

He pulled off her shoes, raised the skirt of her dress and pulled down her panties.

Bending toward her again, he slid his hands up under her thighs to cup her buttocks and pull her toward him.

She was open for him as he leaned in and kissed first one inner thigh and then the other.

Pia quivered and then tensed as he finally laid his mouth against her. Moving at a leisurely pace, he darted and licked with his tongue, and in no time, the room was filled with the sounds of Pia's gasps and moans.

"H-H-Hawk…o-oh!"

Pia tensed and let out a long moan, coming for him.

Only then did Hawk raise his head. She was so unbelievably responsive, he was fighting for control.

Holding her gaze, he undid his shirt and opened his pants, bothering to take off only his shoes. He removed protection from his pocket, sheathed himself and then leaned over her.

It didn't get any more passionate than this, Hawk thought. Lovemaking immediately after work, and they were so randy, they couldn't be bothered to eliminate more than the minimum of clothing.

He couldn't remember being this turned on since he'd been a teenager just discovering sex.

For her part, it was clear that Pia could hardly wait. She slid her hands up his arms in a light caress and arched her body toward him.

They both sighed as he slid inside her.

Hawk fought for control as he felt it slipping. Pia was still as tight as the time he'd taken her virginity.

He could, Hawk thought, lose himself in her again and again.

And in the next moment, he did.

He slid in and out of her, bringing them both mindless pleasure. Coherent thought shut down, and his focus narrowed down to one goal.

He felt Pia gasp and spasm around him with a small climax.

"That's right," he urged hoarsely.

"Hawk, oh, p-please…"

She didn't have to beg. The moment she spoke, a mighty climax shook him. And, dimly but with satisfaction, he was aware of Pia claiming her own peak once again.

With a hoarse groan, he thrust into her one final time, and then slumped against her.

Afterward, they lay on her bed, spent and relaxed. As Pia lay tucked against his side, he caressed her arm.

Since she appeared completely content, he decided to press his advantage.

"Come fishing and riding with me," he said without preamble.

Pia stilled and then stifled a sudden laugh. "You do know how to approach a woman at the right moment." She paused. "Isn't that what we just did?"

He shook his head and responded drolly, "Not that kind."

"Oh?"

"Come fishing and riding with me at Silderly Park in Oxford," he said, naming his ancestral estate in England.

Pia tilted her head to glance up at him.

He knew what he was asking. This had nothing to do with Lucy's wedding anymore. By visiting Silderly Park, Pia would be coming into the heart of who he was as a duke.

He'd made the request unexpectedly, and only belatedly realized how much her answer mattered.

"Yes."

Her answer came out as a breathy whisper before she lowered her head back down to his shoulder.

He smiled slowly, relaxing. "Good."

Pia was his, and he was going to make sure things remained so.

Ten

"The wedding invitations will go out next week," Pia remarked, her comment meant to reassure in case it was necessary.

It was Monday afternoon, and she and Lucy were sitting in the parlor of Hawk's Upper East Side town house. They were meeting over afternoon tea to discuss wedding details.

Most professional shows did not have performances on Monday nights, explaining why it was possible for Lucy to meet with Pia over tea today. Any other day of the week, Lucy might already have been preparing to head to work at this hour.

"Splendid," Lucy said, smoothing her blond hair. "Derek will be happy to know that detail has been taken care of."

It had been a pleasure to work with Hawk's sister, Pia reflected, trying not to dwell on when Hawk might be arriving home.

Lucy and Derek had wanted a relatively simple wedding

ceremony and reception, but one that nevertheless incorporated some nods to Lucy's English ancestry and theater work.

Everything so far had gone smoothly. During previous consultations, the couple had settled on a photographer, band and florist with a minimum of fuss. And today she and Lucy had already discussed wedding music, readings and various ceremony logistics.

"Now the florist has a website," Pia continued, "which you should consult, but in order to give you more ideas, I have my own book of photos from weddings that I've been involved with."

She slid a scrapbook across the coffee table toward Lucy, and Hawk's sister leaned forward and reached for it.

"I'll leave it with you so you can take your time going through it," she added as Lucy opened the book. "You'll see that some brides like more elaborate floral arrangements, and others prefer a simpler concept. Next time we talk, let's discuss what you're looking for before we meet with the florist."

Lucy nodded as she flipped through the scrapbook. "This is helpful." She looked up. "You're so organized, Pia."

"Thank you."

Pia smiled to herself because wedding planners received few acknowledgments of their work. Many brides were too consumed by preparations for their big event to thank the paid help, at least until the wedding was over.

"The other item on our agenda that you should be thinking about now," Pia went on crisply, "is the music that you'd like to be played at the reception."

"Definitely Broadway show tunes," Lucy said with a laugh. "Can I enter on the theme song from *Phantom of the Opera?*"

"You can do whatever you like," Pia responded before a thought intruded that she decided to query about delicately. "Has your mother voiced any opinions?"

In her experience, weddings were fraught with family

negotiations, and often no one had more of an opinion than the mother of the bride. Pia had been called on to referee in more than one instance.

Lucy sighed at Pia's words and sat back, letting the book of photographs fall closed. "Mother means well, but she can be a bit of a dragon, unfortunately."

Pia raised her eyebrows.

"But Hawk doesn't let her have complete free rein." Lucy grinned suddenly. "Of course, it helps that the wedding is happening in New York, thousands of miles from Silderly Park and Mother's back lawn."

In the past, Pia had studiously avoided probing Lucy for more information than she volunteered about her brother. But Lucy had just reminded her of who Pia's de facto employer was, and, as the current duke and head of the family, Hawk undoubtedly had some say in keeping his mother from overriding Lucy's wishes.

In any case, it was a revealing remark on Lucy's part about Carsdale family dynamics.

"Well, it was a deft maneuver to have the wedding here," Pia conceded, "if your intention was to keep interference at a minimum."

Lucy looked sly. "Thank you. It was Derek's idea."

"Ah, right." Pia's lips curved. "He also had the idea of a New Year's wedding, didn't he?"

"Brilliant, isn't it?"

"It's certainly an unorthodox choice."

"I know." Lucy laughed. "I'm sure Mother went absolutely wild. I can picture her pruning her garden with a vengeance after she found out."

A picture popped into Pia's head from Lucy's description, though she'd never met Hawk's mother. She fought an involuntary smile.

"You do have a flair for the dramatic visual, Lucy," she teased. "Anyone would think you should be on the stage."

Lucy gave another laugh. "My first act of rebellion."

"Your family objected?" Pia asked, curiosity getting the better of her.

Lucy's eyes twinkled. "Of course! Mother is well aware that the only actresses in the family tree were all born on the wrong side of the blanket."

Pia was tempted to ask flippantly whether any Carsdale ancestor had kept a wedding planner as a mistress, but she clamped her mouth shut. She wondered, though, how much Lucy knew or suspected about her relationship with Hawk, and what the other woman would say if she knew she was talking to a current lover of the present Duke of Hawkshire.

"Hawk was supportive of me, however," Lucy went on, seemingly oblivious to Pia's reticence. "He's the reason I'm in New York, frankly."

Pia gave a small smile. Lucy clearly thought the world of her brother.

"Speaking of Hawk," Lucy said, "he mentioned you'll be in Oxford and visiting Silderly Park."

Pia hesitated. Just what had Hawk said to Lucy? Did Lucy believe she simply had an incidental interest in touring Silderly Park while she was visiting England, if only because she was planning the wedding of the Duke of Hawkshire's sister?

She had been careful not to discuss Hawk with Lucy because, at first, she hadn't trusted herself to be less than withering in her opinion. And afterward, well, it had become problematic to speak about Hawk...

And, of course, now... Pia heated to think of all the things she *couldn't* bring up with Lucy about how she and Hawk passed the time.

She bit her lip. "Yes, I'm, um, planning to stay at Silderly Park for a few days to fish and ride."

As the words left her mouth, Pia felt a flush crawl up her neck. Drat—would she ever be able to talk about fishing or riding again without blushing?

"Please say you'll stay in Oxford until the first of December then," Lucy pleaded. "It would be so wonderful if you could attend the small engagement party that my mother insisted on hosting at Silderly Park."

"I—"

Pia had never been invited as a guest to a client's wedding function.

"In fact, it would be so nice to have you there."

Pia searched the younger woman's expression, but all she saw there was pure, unguarded appeal.

"I—" Pia cleared her throat and gave a helpless smile. "Okay."

Lucy returned her smile with a grateful one of her own.

Pia wondered whether all the Carsdales were so adamantly persuasive.

Lucy either had no clue about the current state of affairs between her brother and her wedding planner, or, well, she was a very good actress.

In her gossip column, Mrs. Hollings had twice referenced her and Hawk—once right after Belinda's almost-wedding, and more recently, when she'd hinted at a warming of their relationship after Hawk had unexpectedly played her assistant. But Mrs. Hollings had stopped short of naming them as lovers.

And, what's more, Pia wasn't sure if Lucy even paid attention to Mrs. Hollings's column. True, the column included a fair amount of society gossip, but Lucy was immersed in the theater world rather than in the social whirl, and Mrs. Hollings's column focused on New York rather than Britain.

Pia pushed those thoughts aside. "Thank you for the invitation."

Lucy laughed. "Don't be silly. I should be thanking you because you'll be putting up with my mother and my brother."

Ah, yes. *Hawk.*

If Lucy only knew, Pia thought.

Even though her acquaintance with Hawk three years ago had been fleeting—a one-night stand, if she looked at the matter unflinchingly—Pia recognized that he'd changed a lot. He was shouldering a lot more responsibility, and could claim a lot of success through his own hard work. He was also considerate. Look at how he'd tried to help her with her business—insisting on making amends. And she had intimate knowledge that he was a terrific lover.

Still, she couldn't help wondering how Hawk viewed their current sexual interlude. They'd never attempted to attach labels to it. Whatever was the case, though, she insisted to herself, this time she would no longer be the naive and vulnerable young thing.

Lucy regarded her closely. "If you don't mind my saying so, I couldn't help noticing that you and my brother had a testy interaction when you arrived here for our first meeting."

Pia schooled her surprise—Hawk's sister had never brought up that first meeting in prior conversations.

Still, she couldn't deny the truth.

"We did," Pia confessed. "I...didn't form a good opinion of him when I first met him a few years ago."

Now that was a lie. She'd been so taken with him, she'd fallen into bed. It was after their romantic interlude had ended that her opinion of him had soured.

Lucy gave her a small smile. "I can understand why you might not have. I know my brother had his party years, though he never shared the details with me because I was so much younger." She paused, looking at Pia more closely. "But that phase of his life all came to end three years ago."

"Hawk told me," Pia said with sympathy.

Still, Pia got the distinct impression that Lucy meant more than she was saying. Was she trying to persuade Pia that Hawk wasn't so terrible anymore? And if so, why? Because she cared what her wedding planner thought of her brother?

Again, Pia wondered how much Lucy suspected, and what she would say if she knew Pia and Hawk knew each other intimately these days.

Lucy sighed. "I guess there's no going back, is there?" she asked rhetorically. "In any case, Hawk has taken over as head of the family remarkably well. And Sunhill Investments has reversed the state of the ducal finances in just a couple of years—it's remarkable."

Pia fixed a smile. She was reminded of how Hawk had spent his time while he was apparently forgetting her, and an element of doubt intruded again. She was crazy to think she could somehow become remarkable herself—let alone unforgettable—to a man like him. He was a duke and a multimultimillionaire. She was a wedding planner from Pennsylvania.

She pushed back the heart-in-the-throat feeling and convinced herself again that she was prepared for the eventual end of their fling.

Lucy reached out a hand and touched her on the arm. "All I'm saying, Pia, is that Hawk isn't the person that he was even three years ago. You should give him a chance."

Pia wondered what kind of chance Lucy thought she should be giving Hawk. Was she suggesting that Pia should like him enough to interact nicely with him…or more?

Pia opened and closed her mouth.

"All is forgiven," she said finally for Lucy's benefit. "You needn't worry that Hawk and I are unable to get along."

In fact, lately, they'd gotten along so well, they'd gotten into bed together.

"Good," Lucy said with a smile, seemingly accepting her vague answer. "Because I know he likes you. He sang your praises when he suggested you to me as a wedding coordinator."

Pia smiled uncertainly.

She wasn't sure upon what basis Hawk's sister was resting the observation that Hawk *liked* her, but she felt a flutter of happiness at the thought.

Her reaction was both wonderful *and* a cause for concern…

Pia walked beside Hawk in his impressive landscaped gardens.

Since arriving at Hawk's family estate near Oxford two days ago, she and Hawk had gone fishing and riding on his estate, as promised. She'd also been busy working long distance and taking in the many, many rooms that comprised Silderly Park.

She'd tried not to be overwhelmed by the medieval manor house itself. On a previous trip to Britain, she had toured nearby Blenheim Palace, the Duke of Marlborough's family seat. And she could say without a doubt that though Silderly Park didn't carry the identifier in its name, it was no less a palace.

Pia glanced momentarily at the windowed stories of Silderly Park as she and Hawk strolled along and he pointed out various plantings to her. They were both dressed in jackets for the nippy but nevertheless unseasonably warm November weather.

Hawk's principal residence had two wings, and its medieval core had been updated and added to over the centuries. The manor house boasted beautiful painted plaster ceilings, two rooms with magnificent oak paneling and a great hall that could seat 200 or 300 guests. The reception rooms displayed an impressive collection of eighteenth- and nineteenth-century artwork, from various artists, including Gainsborough and Sir Joshua Reynolds.

Even though the income was no longer necessary to him, Hawk had kept Silderly Park open to the public, so that the formal reception rooms could be visited by tourists.

Still, Pia couldn't help feeling as if *she* didn't belong here. Unlike Belinda and Tamara, she hadn't been born to wealth and social position. Maybe if she had, she would have recognized Hawk as more than a plain Mr. James Fielding on the first occasion she'd met him.

"The gardens were created in the late eighteenth century," Hawk said, calling her back from her thoughts. "We use at least five or six different types of rose plantings in the section we're in now."

Pia clasped her hands together in front of her. "This would be a wonderful place to consult for roses to use in weddings. Every bride is looking for something different and unique."

"If you're interested, the gardener could tell you more," Hawk said, sending her a sidelong look. "Or you could come back in the Spring."

Pia felt a shiver of awareness chase down her spine. Was Hawk thinking their relationship would continue at least until Spring—well past Lucy's wedding?

"Perhaps," she forced herself to equivocate, careful not to look at him. "Spring is my busy season for weddings, as you can well imagine."

"Of course, only if you can fit me into your schedule," Hawk teased.

She chanced a glance at him. He looked every inch the lord of the manor in a tweed jacket and wool trousers.

"I'm becoming quite busy these days thanks to you, as you well know," she returned lightly. "I received a call just before we left New York from another friend of yours seeking a wedding coordinator."

Hawk smiled. "I'm hurrying them all to the altar for your sake."

"I'm surprised that you didn't spring for the ring and stage the proposal in this case."

"If I could have, I would have," he said with mock solemnity, "but my expertise lies in locating wedding veils and saving flower bouquets from canine bridal attendants."

Pia laughed, even as she silently acknowledged all of Hawk's help.

With the exception of Tamara's, the weddings that she'd coordinated this past summer had been ones that she'd been contracted for before the Marquess of Easterbridge had crashed Belinda's ill-fated ceremony. Since then, new business had come to her thanks mainly to Hawk.

She had a lot to thank him for, including arranging and paying for both their first-class tickets on a commercial flight from New York to London—though she knew in reality *that* had nothing to do with Lucy's wedding.

She and Hawk came to a stop near some elaborately shaped hedges, and he turned to face her.

He reached out and caressed the line of her jaw, a smile touching his lips.

Pia's senses awakened at his touch, even as time slowed and space narrowed, and her brain turned sluggish.

"D-don't tell me," Pia said, her voice slightly breathless, "that romantic assignations in the gardens are de rigueur."

"If only it wasn't November," he murmured, his eyes crinkling. "Fortunately, there's a bed nearby."

Pia heated as Hawk ducked his head and touched his lips to hers.

She knew the bed to which he was referring. She'd slept in it last night.

Hawk's bedchamber at Silderly Park was in an enormous suite, bigger than her apartment in New York. The suite was fronted by a sitting room, and the bedroom itself boasted a large four-poster bed, red-and-white wallpaper, and gold leaf detail on the molded ceiling.

Everything was fit for a duke.

Everything in Hawk's house, in fact, was out of a fairy tale. Including its owner, Pia thought whimsically.

It was easy to be enthralled, especially for a romantic such as herself…and Pia reminded herself again to keep her feet planted on the ground.

Hawk linked his hand with hers, and Pia allowed him to turn them back in the direction of the house.

Though it was a good fifteen minutes before they arrived at his suite, they snuggled and exchanged the occasional kiss along the way, heedless of whom they might encounter.

In his bedroom, Hawk looked into her eyes as he undressed her, slowly and tenderly, bringing tears to Pia's eyes.

They made love languorously, as if they had not a care in the world, but all the time.

Afterward, Pia lay in Hawk's arms, and sighed with contentment.

"We really have to stop doing this," she remarked.

"What?" Hawk glanced down at her. "Making love in the afternoon?"

"Yes, it's decadent."

"It's the only indulgence I'm allowed these days," Hawk protested. "And my BlackBerry is beeping nearby."

Pia lifted her head and smiled at him. "I'm not used to it."

He raised an eyebrow. "This is beyond your realm of expertise?"

"Oh, Hawk, haven't you guessed?" she asked tentatively.

He stilled, searching her gaze.

"You're my first and only lover." She paused, and then added, "Th-there hasn't been anyone else in the past three years."

Hawk's brows drew together in puzzlement. "You're a desirable woman—"

Pia gave a small, self-conscious laugh, her heart bursting. "I-it wasn't for lack of opportunity, b-but by choice."

Hawk shifted so he was looking down at her as she lay

back. "I don't understand. You've taken the initiative...unlike what I remembered."

"Books and videos," she answered succinctly. "I wanted to educate myself."

So I'd never run the risk of losing you again to lack of experience.

Hawk said nothing for a moment, and Pia gave him a tentative smile.

Hawk's expression softened. "Ah, Pia." He gave her a gentle kiss. "I'm honored."

She arched into him, responding intuitively to his advance.

"So that's why you weren't on any protection when we were first intimate again that day after rock climbing," he murmured.

Pia nodded. "There hadn't been any need."

"That day, you said three years was a long time," Hawk mused. "I thought you were referring to how long it had been since we'd last been together. But you meant since the last time you'd had sex, too, didn't you?"

Pia nodded again, and then her eyes crinkled. "Care to shorten the time between sex?"

Hawk gave a half groan, half laugh. "Ah, Pia. It's going to be difficult to keep up with you."

She gave him a quick kiss, her look mischievous. "Your performance has been off the charts so far. I thought—"

"Minx." He silenced her with a kiss.

And after that, neither of them got out of bed for a long while.

Hawk knew he was in too deep.

It was déjà vu. Except the first time he hadn't suspected that Pia was a virgin, and this time, he hadn't divined that she'd only ever had one lover. *Him.*

He felt a rush of possessiveness. He hadn't liked thinking

of Pia with other men—learning things...things that *he* could teach her.

Blast it.

"What do you think, Hawk?"

Hawk met three pairs of expectant female eyes. His mother, his sister and Pia were sitting in the Green Room at Silderly Park discussing assorted wedding details. He'd assumed a position by the mantel, at a safe remove.

"What do you think about seating Baron Worling next to Princess Adelaide of Meznia at dinner?" his mother asked, repeating and elaborating her question.

Hawk knew there was some nuance that he should understand, otherwise his mother wouldn't have bothered asking. But for the life of him, he couldn't think what it was.

Was Baron Worling a poor conversationalist? Did Princess Adelaide believe the baron was beneath her notice? Or perhaps one of the baron's poor ancestors had dueled to the death with a member of Princess Adelaide's royal family?

Hawk shrugged and punted. "I'm sure whatever you decide will be fine."

His mother looked nonplussed.

"What about placing the Crown Prince of Belagia on Princess Adelaide's left?" Pia suggested.

His mother brightened. "Splendid idea."

Hawk shot Pia a grateful look.

She looked superb in a navy polka-dot dress and heels. The dress accentuated her bust without being over the top, so that she looked demure but professional.

Whether Pia knew it or not, Hawk reflected, she'd chosen exactly an outfit of which his mother, the Dowager Duchess of Hawkshire, would approve.

As the wedding conversation resumed, Hawk started idly plotting ways to be alone again with Pia.

Could he invent a phone call that required her immediate

attention and called her away? Or perhaps he could feign a pressing need for her to consult on his attire for the wedding day? He stifled a grin.

Yesterday they had gone horseback riding and he'd shown her the various natural and architectural wonders on his estate. He couldn't remember when he'd enjoyed playing tour guide more, though he had an understandable bit of pride in his ancestral estate and childhood home.

His mother glanced up and caught his eye, and Hawk returned her look blandly.

He wondered whether his mother suspected that there was more than a business relationship between him and Lucy's wedding planner, and decided to leave her to speculate. He and Pia had separate bedrooms, and they'd been discreet about their late-night rendezvous, even though Silderly Park was so large that it was unlikely they'd have attracted the attention of anyone while slipping in and out of each other's rooms.

The truth was, he was still trying to sort out his feelings and next steps as far as Pia was concerned. How could he articulate them for someone else when he himself didn't understand them?

He'd started out trying to make amends, true, but matters had gotten more complicated from there. He bore a large share of the responsibility for his current circumstances—mostly because he couldn't seem to help himself as far as Pia was concerned. He must have been absent that day in grade school when they taught everyone about keeping their hands to themselves.

He was Pia's first and *only* lover.

It was astounding. It was wonderful.

It also made him freeze, not knowing what to do.

For years, his code of conduct with respect to women was never to get too involved. It was the reason why he'd never been or wanted to be a woman's first lover—until Pia.

And while he still wasn't sure about many things, he did know that he didn't want to see Pia hurt again.

The butler entered, followed by a familiar-looking brunette.

Hawk watched as his mother brightened, and as recognition set in, he was struck with an impending sense of doom, even before the butler spoke.

"Miss Michelene Ward-Fombley has arrived."

Eleven

Pia looked up as an attractive brunette walked into the room, and immediately and inexplicably sensed that something was wrong.

The Dowager Duchess of Hawkshire, however, rose gracefully from her seat on the settee, a smile wreathing her face. "Michelene, darling, how lovely of you to join us here."

Michelene stepped forward, and the two women exchanged air kisses.

Pia glanced around the room, noticing that Lucy had a worried expression while Hawk was still as a rock by the mantel.

Following Lucy's lead, Pia rose from her seat as introductions were made.

"...and this is Miss Pia Lumley, who has been ever so helpful as Lucy's wedding coordinator," the duchess said with a smile.

Pia shook hands with Michelene, whom she pegged as a

cool self-possessed blueblood. Though the other woman had said only a few words, Pia could tell that Michelene spoke Queen's English with a distinctive upper-class inflection.

Michelene looked over at the mantel.

"Hawk," Michelene murmured, her voice low and sultry.

Hawk? *Not Your Grace?* Pia frowned. Exactly what was the status of the relationship between Michelene and Hawk?

Pia knew that never in a million years—not even in the shower—could she imitate Michelene's smoky tone. She even stuttered during sex—for which she was self-conscious, though Hawk claimed to like it.

"Michelene," Hawk acknowledged, remaining at his spot by the mantel. "How nice to see you. I wasn't made aware that you were coming today."

Pia watched as Hawk threw his mother a meaningful look, which the dowager duchess returned with one—Pia could swear—of the cat who ate the canary. Score one for the dowager, it seemed.

"Did I not mention that Michelene was arriving early for Lucy's engagement party tomorrow?" the duchess said, raising her brows. "Oh, dear."

Michelene gave a little laugh. "I hope it's no inconvenience."

"Not at all. You are more than welcome here," Hawk said smoothly, his eyes traveling from Michelene to his mother. "Silderly Park is large enough, of course, to accommodate the occasional unexpected guest."

Whoever Michelene was, Pia thought, it was clear that she was close to the Carsdales.

Was she, in fact, a former lover of Hawk's? Pia tamped down the well of jealousy.

"We were just finishing up our discussion of the wedding," the duchess said as she sat back down. "Won't you join us, Michelene?"

Pia and Lucy followed the duchess's lead in retaking their seats.

"Thank you," Michelene said as she sat down as well. "I believe I would find listening to be vastly informative." She smiled toward the side of the room where Hawk was standing. "There was a time when I imagined I'd enjoy becoming a wedding planner myself. Unfortunately, life had other plans, and I remained in the fashion business."

Pia shifted uncomfortably. She wondered whether Hawk and Michelene had not only been lovers, but had come close to a walk down the aisle. Or perhaps Michelene had hoped for a marriage proposal that had never materialized, and Hawk had ended the relationship instead?

Pia mentally braked. She knew she was letting her imagination run away with her. She had no proof that Hawk and Michelene had even dated, let alone come close to marriage. And she was making an assumption that Hawk had ended any relationship between the two.

"Wh-what type of fashion?" Pia blurted, disconcerted by her thoughts.

A second later, she clamped her mouth shut. She was embarrassed by the sudden and unexpected appearance of her stutter. She must be more rattled than she realized.

Michelene looked at her keenly. "I'm a buyer for Harvey Nichols."

Pia was familiar with the upmarket department store. She just wished she could afford more of their goods.

"It must be so interesting to be a wedding planner," Michelene continued, hitting the ball back into Pia's court. "You must have some entertaining stories."

This year more than others, Pia thought.

"I do enjoy the job very much," she nevertheless responded honestly. "I love being part of one of the most significant days in a couple's life."

Pia could feel Hawk's gaze on her, his expression thoughtful.

"Pia has been a great help," Lucy put in with an encouraging smile.

"I see," Michelene said. "I'll have to get your business card, Ms. Lumley—"

"It's Pia, please."

"—just in case anyone I know is in need of the services of a wedding coordinator."

Pia again got the sense there was a subtext to this conversation that she wasn't privy to.

Before she could say anything else, however, the butler appeared again to announce that Lucy's dressmaker—the one Pia knew had been commissioned to make a suitable confection for the engagement party—had arrived.

As the dressmaker was shown in, Pia cast a speculative look at Hawk's enigmatic expression.

She wondered if she'd be able to learn the subtext of today's conversation sooner rather than later. Because she *and* Hawk would no doubt be seeing Michelene again tomorrow at Lucy's engagement party.

Pia surveyed the glittering crowd from her position near one end of the long dining table, one of two that had been set up parallel to each other in the Great Hall.

There would be dinner and dancing for the engagement party tonight, as befitted a formal reception given by a dowager duchess, since Hawk's mother was playing hostess. The men wore tuxes, and the women gowns.

Lucy had dismissed all of tonight's pomp and circumstance as more of a to-do than the wedding itself would be. But she had conceded that her mother should have a free hand tonight if the dowager duchess was to have very little say over the wedding itself.

Pia had donned one of the two floor-length gowns that she

owned. The nature of her line of work required her to dress very formally on occasion.

She wore a lavender, one-shoulder, Grecian-style dress whose artfully draped fabric accentuated her bust and gave her the illusion of additional height. She'd bought the designer Marchesa gown at an Upper East Side consignment shop that was a favorite with the rich and fashionable who looked to retire their clothes at the end of the season.

As she cut into her remaining filet mignon—during a momentary lull in conversation with the guests seated to her right and left—she shot a surreptitious look down the middle of the table at Hawk.

He looked handsome and debonair as he chatted with the graying man to his left—a prince of some long-defunct kingdom, if she recalled correctly, who also happened to be distantly related to Derek, Lucy's fiancé.

She herself sat far away from Hawk, near one end of the table, as befitted her position as a less notable guest—an employee, really, and no more, in the dowager duchess's eyes.

She couldn't help but note that Michelene, on the other hand, had been seated diagonally across from Hawk—within speaking distance.

She wished she'd questioned Hawk about the other woman, but, truth be told, she'd been afraid of the answers. She hadn't wanted her suspicions confirmed that Michelene and Hawk had been more than friends at one point. And Hawk hadn't volunteered any information.

Pia patted her mouth with her napkin and took a sip of her wine.

As waiters began clearing plates from the table, Hawk rose and a hush fell over the room.

Pia kept her gaze on him, even though his own eyes traveled over the room, surveying the assembled guests.

Hawk said a few short words, thanking all the guests for

joining his family in tonight's celebration and regaling the crowd with a couple of amusing anecdotes about his sister and future brother-in-law. Then he toasted the happy couple and all the assembled guests joined in.

When he took his seat again, the dowager duchess rose from hers. She gave the engaged couple seated near her an indulgent smile. "I'm so very happy for Lucy and Derek."

Hawk's mother cleared her throat. "As many of you know, Lucy hasn't always followed my advice—" there was a scattering of laughter among the guests "—but in this case she has my unqualified approval." She raised her glass. "Well done, Lucy, and it is with great pleasure that I welcome you to the family, Derek."

"Hear, hear," chorused some of the guests.

The duchess lifted her glass higher. "I hope I shall have the opportunity to make another toast on a similarly happy occasion in the not-too-distant future." Her gaze shifted for a moment to Hawk before returning to her daughter and future son-in-law. "To Lucy and Derek."

As everyone raised their glasses in toast and sipped their champagne, Pia watched as the dowager duchess's gaze came to rest on Michelene. In turn, the younger woman glanced at Hawk, who was gazing at his mother, his expression inscrutable.

Pia felt her stomach plummet.

Sightlessly, she placed her glass back on the table without taking a sip.

Feeling suddenly ill, she experienced an overwhelming need to get away—to get some air.

Pia murmured an excuse in the general direction of her nearest dinner companions and rose from her seat.

Trying not to catch anyone's eye, she hurried from the room as fast as decorum would allow.

In the hall, she ran up the stairs. She was roiled by emotion that threatened to spill over into tears.

She'd been so naive yesterday. It was something that she'd

vowed to herself she'd never be again. And yet, she'd mistaken the situation entirely.

It wasn't that Michelene and Hawk had a *past* relationship that had been broken off. It was that they had a *current* tie that had an expectation of marriage.

Pia had gathered as much from the interchange that had just occurred during the dowager duchess's speech, and from the significant looks that had been exchanged.

She'd finally pieced together yesterday's puzzle, but in the process, she'd nearly humiliated herself in front of dozens of people.

At the top of the stairs, she turned left. Her bedroom was down the hallway.

"Pia, wait."

Hawk's voice came from behind her, more command than plea. He sounded as if he was taking the stairs two at a time.

She picked up her pace. She hoped to reach the sanctuary of her room and throw the lock before he caught up with her. It was her only hope. She didn't want to risk having him see her break down.

She could hear Hawk's rapid steps behind her. In her gown, she couldn't move as fast as he could, though she had the hem raised with one hand.

And in the next moment, it was too late.

Hawk caught up with her, grasping her arm and turning her to face him.

"Wh-what?" she demanded, her throat clogged. "It's not midnight yet and C-Cinderella isn't allowed to disappear, is that it?"

"Are you leaving behind a glass slipper?" he countered, dropping his staying hand.

She gave an emotional laugh. "No, and you're not Prince Charming."

His lips firmed into a thin line. "Let's go somewhere and discuss this."

At least he understood why she was upset, and he wasn't going to pretend otherwise.

Still. "I'm not going anywhere with you!"

Hawk sighed. "Will you let me explain?"

"D-damn you, Hawk," she said, her voice wobbly. "I—I was just starting to trust you again! Now I discover that all along you've more or less had a fiancée waiting in the wings."

Pia's jaw clenched. Did he know how fragile trust was? How could she ever trust him again?

He looked her in the eye. "That's what my mother would like to believe."

"Oh? And you were unaware of this expectation?"

He remained silent.

Obviously, he was refusing to incriminate himself, Pia thought acerbically. He knew anything he said could and would be used against him.

"It appears that your mother had more than an expectation."

Michelene herself obviously did, too. And Pia recalled Lucy's troubled expression yesterday in the Green Room. Had Hawk's sister realized that Michelene's unexpected appearance would present an awkward situation for her brother?

Hawk muttered something under his breath.

"You and Michelene seemed quite familiar yesterday!"

"You're mistaking matters or else deliberately mis-characterizing them," he responded in a clipped tone. "I recall remaining by the fireplace when Michelene appeared."

"You know what I mean," Pia said, feeling like stamping her foot—as childish as that might be. "And why should I believe anything that you tell me? You failed to mention Michelene's existence to begin with."

"I was involved with Michelene briefly after my brother's death. Michelene had been considered an eligible candidate to be my brother's future duchess." Hawk shrugged. "I was stepping into my brother's shoes, and Michelene was part of the package."

And Pia wasn't. She could hear the words as clearly as if they'd been spoken aloud.

As Hawk trailed off, Pia acknowledged the situation that he'd been in. He'd fallen into doing what had been expected of him. She could almost understand that.

And yet. "Your mother acts as if an engagement announcement is imminent. If I hadn't stayed for the party at Lucy's request, is that how I would have heard about Michelene? An engagement notice in the paper?"

Hawk's engagement to another woman. She couldn't help feeling hurt as well as betrayed. She'd told herself she'd be prepared for the end of their affair, but she hadn't foreseen *this.*

"I am not engaged, I assure you," Hawk shot back, looking frustrated. "I hadn't planned a proposal or bought a ring."

"Well, then, you're running late," she replied. "Michelene is waiting."

She glanced down the hall. Someone could come at any time, interrupting and witnessing their argument. And he had to get back downstairs to the party. His absence would be noticed soon.

"Pia, you are the damnedest fe—"

"That's right I—I am," she responded. "I happen to be cursed with rotten luck as far as men are concerned. So much for fairy tales!"

"If you'll just give me a chance—"

"That's the problem," Pia tossed back. "I have."

She turned and started down the hall. "I can't believe I was charmed a-and tricked by you again. How could I have let myself be such a fool?"

Hawk caught up with her and took hold of her arm again, forcing her to look up at him.

His face was set and implacable, and Pia got a glimpse of the part of him that had made a fortune in the span of a few short years.

"I did not trick you," he grated.

A moment later, his lips came down on hers. The kiss packed all the potency of their past ones and then some.

She tasted the champagne on his lips, and inhaled the male scent of him. It was a combination heady enough to make her head swim, despite her anger.

Still, summoning an effort of will, she pulled away as soon as the kiss tapered off.

"You didn't trick me?" she inquired, repeating his words as he raised his head. "Perhaps not. I suppose I tricked myself. All you did was let me."

Hawk looked at her, eyes glittering.

She read her own meaning in his silence.

"I didn't think you approached me again with the idea of a marriage proposal," she scoffed, though she was willing the tears away with all her might.

Hawk searched her eyes. "You know why I approached you…"

Yes, to make amends.

"Pia—"

"I-it's t-too late, Hawk," she said, her voice agonized. "The cat's out of the bag, and we're finished. Our affair was going to have to end sometime, so why not now? Except this time, I'm the one walking away."

Before Hawk could respond, someone called his name, and she and Hawk turned as one to glance down the hall.

Michelene was standing at the top of the stairs.

Not waiting for more, Pia turned and hurried down the hall in the opposite direction, leaving Hawk standing where he was.

Pia slipped inside her bedroom and closed and locked the

door behind her. Then she leaned back against the wall of the darkened room, grateful for reaching sanctuary.

When all of this had started, Hawk's motivation was to make amends. His motivation had never been, she reminded herself, swallowing hard, to love her or promise forever more.

She bit her lip to stop it from trembling, even as the tears welled.

The only question was how was she going to mend her heart when this was over and she'd truly gotten away—if she ever could?

Twelve

As it turned out, Pia managed to make her escape more expeditiously than she'd imagined possible. After collecting herself and drying her tears, she packed her few bags in a hurry and summoned one of Hawk's chauffeurs to drive her to nearby Oxford.

She knew Hawk would remain occupied tonight with the engagement party, whether he liked it or not. She also knew Oxford would afford her a host of inns and hotels in which to stay for the night while she booked a flight back to New York—and planned her next move.

During the night at a small inn, however she remembered that the Earl and Countess of Melton were staying at their home, Gantswood Hall, in nearby Gloucestershire. So the morning, after a quick ring to Tamara, Pia used a rental car to drive to Gantswood Hall.

When Pia arrived after midday, Tamara greeted her inside the front door with a quick hug.

Before she'd left New York, Pia had mentioned to Tamara

that she planned to be in England for Lucy Carsdale's engagement party, so her friend was aware that she would be in the country.

But Pia had said nothing on the phone about the reason for her sudden trip to Gantswood Hall. And if Tamara had been surprised at Pia's impromptu plan to visit, she hadn't given any indication.

Now, as she and Tamara drew apart from their hug, Pia couldn't help experiencing a pang. She'd noticed that her friend's pregnancy had started to show. And Tamara looked happy and relaxed, dressed in a cowl-neck cashmere sweater and black tights, her red hair pulled back in a knot.

Pia knew her own situation was in startling contrast. She couldn't be further away from Tamara's happily-ever-after. She was sad and depressed, and she hadn't slept well last night. No amount of makeup this morning had been able to disguise her pallor and the peaked look around her eyes.

Tamara searched her face, her brow puckering. "What's wrong? You gave no indication on the phone. But I can see from the look of you that something is amiss."

Pia parted her lips. *What was the use in hiding the truth?*

"L-last night was Lucy Carsdale's engagement party," she said without preamble.

Tamara's eyes widened. "Did something go wrong? Oh, Pia!"

Much to her horror, Pia felt her eyes well with tears.

Tamara looked at her with concern for a moment, and then wrapped her in a hug again.

"It's okay," Tamara said soothingly, patting her on the back. "I've been prone to tears myself, what with raging hormones during this pregnancy. I'm sure whatever happened is not as bad as it seems right now."

Pia hiccupped and straightened, taking a step back. "No, it's worse."

Tamara had obviously concluded that Pia was upset because something had gone wrong with Lucy's engagement party, Pia realized. Tamara had no idea about Hawk's role.

When she'd told Tamara and Belinda that she'd be traveling to England in order to help with Lucy's engagement party, she'd left out that Hawk himself had extended an invitation to visit Silderly Park.

Tamara put an arm around her shoulders. "Come into the drawing room with me. We can be cozy there, and you can tell me all about it. I was about to have a light snack brought in."

As a member of the household staff appeared from the back of the house, Tamara added, "Haines, could you please arrange to have Pia's bags moved from her car to the Green and Gold Bedroom? Thank you."

"Of course," Haines acknowledged with an inclination of the head as they passed him.

Pia let Tamara guide her through the palatial house, Sawyer's ancestral family seat, until they reached a large room with French doors overlooking the back lawn and gardens. Despite the masterpieces framed on the walls, the room was warm and inviting.

Pia sat with Tamara on a brocade settee in front of a large fireplace.

Tamara handed her a tissue, and Pia made use of it to compose herself.

"Now," Tamara said encouragingly, "I'm sure this is nothing that you can't put behind you."

Pia bit her lip. *If only Tamara knew.*

"I don't know," she said. "I've been trying to put Hawk behind me for three years."

Tamara's eyebrows lifted. "Then all this emotion isn't because something went wrong with Lucy's engagement party?"

"Oh, something went wrong, all right. I found out Hawk had a fiancée waiting in the wings."

"Oh, Pia."

With some effort, Pia outlined what had happened at Silderly Park—from Michelene's unexpected arrival to what had transpired the night before at Lucy's party.

When she finished, she looked at Tamara beseechingly.

"How could I have been so stupid again?" she asked in an agonized voice. "How could I let myself become vulnerable to him once more?"

"You let yourself become susceptible to Hawk's charms…"

Tamara trailed off, and though she'd spoken without inflection, she seemed to be trying to guess at what Pia was really saying.

Pia sighed. Why not come out with the whole bald-faced truth?

She hadn't divulged details to Tamara and Belinda of her recent and evolving relationship with Hawk. She knew they would have tried to dissuade her from any deeper involvement—and certainly from trying to turn the tables in a high-stakes game with a seasoned player like Hawk.

"It's worse," Pia said succinctly. "I slept with him."

Tamara looked surprised, though not as caught unawares as Pia would have expected. Still, her friend didn't say anything.

"After the first time I slept with him, he disappeared for three years," Pia said, the words tumbling out of her. "This time, we sleep together, and then I discover he's nearly engaged to another woman!"

"Oh, Pia," Tamara said. "I had no idea, believe me. If I'd known, of course I would have said something."

Tamara frowned. "I wonder why Sawyer didn't say anything. He and Hawk are friends. He must have had at least some inkling about an engagement—"

Pia shrugged. "Perhaps Sawyer had no idea that a warning

was necessary. I mean, Hawk and I had a past but no present. And now, we definitely have no future…"

Pia felt a wave of pain wash over her. Had she started hoping for a future with Hawk? How much of her hurt was due to the fact that she really hadn't wanted the relationship to end, and how much due to the way she'd shockingly found out that it was over—because there was another woman?

It shouldn't hurt this bad.

If she was honest with herself, she'd say she'd never completely gotten over Hawk. And now…now she was in love with him while he was going to marry another woman.

The realization hit like a body blow.

"Pia?" Tamara said. "Are you okay?"

Pia could only nod, her throat too constricted for words.

Tamara stroked her arm soothingly. "I know it hurts. You'll need time."

Pia nodded, and then took a deep breath.

"I was so naive," she announced when she could speak again. "When Michelene arrived, I thought perhaps she and Hawk had dated in the past. It never occurred to me that I should be concerned about the future!"

"Well, don't worry. I'll have Sawyer call Hawk out," Tamara stated, trying to lighten the mood. "Sawyer must have some centuries-old ceremonial swords lying around somewhere that they can duel with…"

Pia gave a choked laugh. "I don't know. Hawk is in good shape. He's a rock climber."

Pia was thankful for Tamara's understanding. She wasn't sure if Belinda would have managed to be quite so deft at a time like this. But then Tamara was happily married, while Belinda was trying her utmost to be happily *unmarried*.

Pia tried to compose herself, and gave Tamara a watery smile. "Thanks for trying to cheer me up."

Tamara gave a rueful little smile of her own. "I know what

you're going through, Pia, believe me. It's where I was just a few months ago."

"But everything worked out for you. Sawyer adores you."

"I didn't think it was possible at the time. There'll come a day when you'll be happy again—I promise."

Pia sighed. "Not any time soon. I'm committed to seeing through Lucy's big event. How will it look if I end this horrible year by dropping Lucy's wedding at the last moment? It will truly be a fatal blow to Pia Lumley Wedding Productions!"

Tamara grimaced. "I wish I could question Sawyer right now, but he flew back to New York yesterday, and I know he's in a business meeting right now."

"It's okay. It won't change anything."

Nothing could make this right.

"What is Michelene's full name?" Tamara queried suddenly.

"It's Ward-Fombley. Michelene Ward-Fombley."

Tamara nodded. "I've heard of her, though I can't put a face to the name at the moment."

"She's genteel and attractive."

"So are you."

"You're loyal."

Tamara tilted her head. "I'm sure I've heard the name in connection with one social function or another here in England…"

"I'm not surprised," Pia admitted, though it hurt. "She's from Hawk's social circle. In fact, I believe she was a leading candidate to be Hawk's older brother's bride until William passed away."

Tamara grimaced again. "Oh, Pia, are you sure Hawk isn't just feeling some lingering halfhearted sense of obligation?"

"Even if he is, it doesn't change matters. He engaged in some artful omissions, and I can only assume that his sense of obligation remains."

Hawk had assumed responsibilities in the past three years, Pia reflected, and she was suffering the consequences.

She recalled the look on the dowager duchess's face last night. Yes, Pia thought with a stab, Hawk had his life mapped out for him, and their paths were apparently fated to cross only briefly and casually, with no serious feelings or commitment—at least not on his part.

"I need to book a flight," Pia told Tamara. "With any luck, I can catch a plane back to New York by tomorrow."

Her friend looked troubled. "Oh, Pia, please stay longer. You're upset."

Pia was glad for the offer, but still she shook her head. "Thank you, Tamara—for everything." She pasted on a brave smile. "But I have business that needs attending to back in New York."

At the moment, she added silently, she needed to put as much space as possible between her and Hawk.

She also worried that if Sawyer returned home, he'd inform Hawk of her whereabouts. Pia had come to like Tamara's husband, but she knew he was also Hawk's friend.

And she wasn't ready to face Hawk again quite so soon.

Once she was back in New York, she only had to figure out how to avoid Hawk until Lucy's wedding was over. Because one thing was certain—they were over as a couple.

Hawk sat in his office in New York in a rare quiet moment and reflected on the royal mess he'd made.

Pia had run from him, and he no doubt ranked even lower than the fictional wicked Mr. Wickham in her estimation at the moment.

Mrs. Hollings, no doubt using her crystal ball and her contacts across the Atlantic, had published more or less the heart of the matter in her column: "Could a certain rakish, hawkish duke have resurrected his randy dandy ways before heading to the altar with a suitable marriageable miss?"

His painstakingly built reputation as a serious financier with hardly a remarkable social life was threatening to collapse. He'd merited three thinly-veiled references in Mrs. Hollings's gossip column in the past months.

Pia had laid dust to his resolve to appear—and to *be*— strictly proper and responsible. He'd thought he was reformed. She'd proved him wrong.

She thought he'd played her false, and the truth was, he'd been less than aboveboard and forthright. As a result, Pia had been crushed by the unexpected events at Lucy's engagement party.

And Mrs. Hollings, blast it, knew it all.

It would be easy, of course, for him to track down Pia. He knew where she lived, and she was still working on Lucy's wedding—or rather, he thought she was.

Lucy had become rather tight-lipped on the subject of Pia. His sister had seemed to intuit what had transpired at Silderly Park, based on Michelene's unexpected arrival and Pia's abrupt departure. It was clear that Lucy disapproved of his treatment of Pia, though she'd refrained from outright verbal censuring.

And then again, what would he say to Pia if he tracked her down?

He should have told her about Michelene and *explained*— but what exactly? Until Pia had unexpectedly reappeared in his life on Belinda's wedding day in June, he and everyone else had thought he'd marry someone suitable. It had been, in so many ways, the path of least resistance. It was time to marry, and with his reputation as a top-flight financier in place, a predictable marriage had been the final step toward burying his playboy past for good.

Yet how serious could he ever have been about Michelene if she'd barely even crossed his mind the whole time he'd been with Pia? He asked himself that question now. The idea of proposing to Michelene had never assumed concrete terms…

When the phone rang, he leaned forward and picked up the receiver on his desk. "Yes?"

"Sawyer Langsford is here to see you."

"Tell him to come in."

After replacing the phone, he rose from his chair, just in time to see Sawyer walk into his office.

As Hawk came around his desk, he was glad to see his friend, even though he had some suspicion as to what had precipitated this visit.

"If you're here to castigate me," he said without preamble, "I can assure you that I'm already doing a fine job of it myself."

Sawyer smiled wryly. "Tamara suggested a duel at dawn, but I set her straight that it wasn't quite the thing anymore among us aristocrats."

"Good Lord, I should hope not," Hawk muttered as he shook hands with Sawyer. "I don't think my mother would take kindly to the dukedom passing into the hands of a distant cousin for lack of male heirs."

Sawyer's eyes crinkled.

Hawk nodded at one of the chairs set before his desk. "Have a seat."

Sawyer sat down, and Hawk went back around his desk and reclaimed his chair.

Sawyer's lips twisted into a sardonic smile. "My impression actually was that you were doing your utmost to sire an heir."

Hawk wasn't sure if Sawyer was referring to his liaison with Pia or rumors of his prospective proposal to Michelene. In any case, it hardly mattered.

"Ah, yes, the heart of the matter," Hawk said, steepling his fingers. "This is what has gotten me into hot water. Even your Mrs. Hollings is apparently on to the story."

Sawyer shrugged. "What can I say? Mrs. Hollings's realm extends even beyond my reach."

"Obviously."

"Much as I hate to point out the obvious," Sawyer said, "Mrs. Hollings was reporting a story of your own creation."

Hawk sighed, acknowledging the truth of Sawyer's statement. "Much to my regret."

Sawyer smiled. "In any case, my pretext for coming here was to extend an apology in person for your name's appearance in the wrong section of one of my newspapers."

Hawk inclined his head in mock solemnity. "Thank you. Far better than a duel at dawn."

"Quite." Sawyer arched a brow. "I did caution you about Pia."

"Yes, I recall," Hawk replied. "And I proceeded heedlessly. Obviously, I'm an inconsiderate libertine of the first order. A debaucher of innocence."

In fact, these days he found himself questioning what his intentions had been all along. Had he been disingenuous? And even if his intentions had been good, they now lay like flotsam on the shore.

Sawyer inclined his head. "You can always be reformed."

"I thought I was."

Sawyer gave a hint of a smile. "Again, then. You're the only one who can fix this situation."

Hawk twisted his lips. "How? I've been racking my brain and have yet to come up with a solution."

"You will," Sawyer replied. "I was sitting where you are only a few months ago, thinking similar thoughts about Tamara. Except that you came into your title unexpectedly as a younger son, unlike me and Easterbridge. You had less time to get accustomed to it. All I'll say is, yes, the title is a responsibility, but don't let yourself get overburdened by it. Think about what makes you happy rather than what's suitable."

Hawk nodded, surprised by Sawyer's insight, though maybe he shouldn't have been.

Sawyer's lips tilted upward. "And lastly, women appreciate grand gestures." He checked his watch. "Now, if you're free, let's have lunch."

Hawk shook his head in amused disbelief as he and Sawyer both rose from their seats. He'd had enough of grand gestures. Look where they'd landed him.

Still, he would venture to guess that Sawyer was correct.

Thirteen

Pia had decided to lie low.

She wasn't sure where and how Mrs. Hollings was getting her information, but the columnist seemed to have sources in the most unlikely of places.

In fact, Pia wondered fancifully for a moment if Mrs. Hollings had been able to bribe information out of Mr. Darcy. Mr. Darcy was known to be a pushover for having his tummy rubbed or for a handful of kitty treats.

As she moved along Broadway from the subway to her destination—jostled occasionally on the crowded street by a passerby or tourist—she noted that it was an unusually bright December day. *So unlike her mood.*

She'd suggested to Lucy that they meet in her dressing room before her performance tonight. She didn't want to run the risk of encountering Hawk at his house.

She didn't want to face him until she was ready, which might be never.

Still, though it was nonsensical, at the same time she missed Hawk terribly.

He appeared to be giving her a wide berth—it was the only way to explain why she hadn't heard from him. He could have tracked her down. He knew where she lived.

She was almost annoyed with him for *not* tracking her down. If he cared, wouldn't he beat a path to her door to mount a defense, however feeble?

Pia sighed. She ought to have hardened her heart against Hawk since their last confrontation. Instead, she was a mass of incredibly conflicted feelings.

Perhaps she was a pushover and always would be. She'd learned nothing, clearly, about eradicating her trusting nature and protecting her too-easily-bruised feelings.

Arriving at the Drury Theater, she went in the front entrance and was directed to Lucy's dressing room.

When she knocked on Lucy's partially-open dressing room door and then entered, Hawk's sister swiveled in her chair to face her.

"Pia!" Lucy rose and came over to give her a quick squeeze. "You're right on time."

She might have had a falling-out with Hawk, but Pia continued to like Lucy. The other woman's enthusiasm was almost contagious. And though this wasn't usually the case with her clients, she believed that she and Lucy had become friends of sorts over the past few months.

"Hardly anyone is here, since it's hours until curtain time," Lucy said as she stepped back. "Can I offer you something to drink? Tea—" Lucy's eyes sparkled with humor "—or maybe coffee or hot chocolate?"

"No, please," she declined. "I'm fine at the moment."

She removed her hat and coat, and Lucy took them and her purse from her to place on a nearby coatrack.

As they both sat down in vacant chairs, Pia looked around the smallish room. It boasted a mirrored dressing table lit by naked bulbs and strewn with an array of makeup and hair preparation items. There was also the coatrack, a few chairs and plenty of discarded wardrobe items.

Pia let her gaze come back to Lucy, and she smiled encouragingly. "You are one of the calmest brides whom I have ever worked with."

Lucy laughed. "I suppose I'd be more nervous if work wasn't keeping me so busy. But then I'm used to performing in front of people, and isn't a wedding a type of performance?"

"I suppose that explains it."

Lucy looked at her thoughtfully. "I want to thank you for attending the engagement party at Silderly Park. You left so soon, I didn't have time to say anything."

"Yes, well…" Pia found it hard to hold Lucy's gaze. "It was my pleasure."

Lucy tilted her head. "I don't suppose your abrupt departure had anything to do with Hawk and Michelene?"

Pia was startled by the direct question, and for a moment, she wasn't sure she'd heard correctly.

"Wh-what makes you ask that?" she said, eyes wide.

She flushed to think about how many of the other guests at the engagement party had surmised what happened.

Lucy smiled understandingly. "When it's your brother, and you're on the verge of getting married yourself, you notice things."

"You needn't worry," she tried gamely. "I'm well-prepared to deal with Michelene and H-Hawk's w-wedding plans."

"Pia…"

She fought to hold on to her composure. How humiliating would it be to break down in front of Hawk's sister, and to have Lucy tell Hawk about it?

Lucy's smile flickered, comprehension in her eyes. "If it helps, I'm convinced Hawk cares about you. Very much."

If he cared, Pia thought, he would have told her about Michelene instead of having her discover the other woman's position in his life in such a public way. If he cared, he would have called or contacted her.

If he cared, he wouldn't be so charming and easy to fall in love with.

Good grief, she thought, was there no end to Hawk's ability to toy with her life?

Lucy sighed. "I believe Michelene's arrival caught Hawk by surprise as much as it did you."

Pia thinned her lips. "I'm sure it did. I can just imagine what an uncomfortable position Michelene put him in. He suddenly had his current lover and his future wife under the same roof, and they weren't the same woman!"

Then she belatedly clamped her mouth shut, afraid she'd said too much.

Lucy grimaced. "Hawk has an amazing ability to muck things up, sometimes."

"Sometimes?" Pia queried, regaining some of her aplomb. "You know the first time I met him he presented himself as plain Mr. James Fielding?"

"So the rumors are true," Lucy murmured, as if speaking to herself.

Pia had wondered how much Lucy realized or suspected about her relationship with Hawk. Now she had her answer.

Lucy searched Pia's face, her own reflecting worry. "I've never seen Hawk as happy as he is with you. Please take that for what it's worth."

There was a part of her that yearned to believe Lucy's words. She was already a mix of conflicted feelings.

"Do you know he spoke glowingly of you when he suggested I use you as my wedding coordinator?" Lucy went on. "I could see from his face that you weren't a mere acquaintance. I could tell there was more he wasn't telling me."

Pia felt herself flush. "H-he told me he wanted to make amends for the past..."

"And he mucked up the setting-to-right part, too," Lucy guessed, finishing for her.

Pia nodded. "He didn't mention Michelene." She swallowed against the sudden lump in her throat. "But I should have known there'd be someone like her waiting in the wings. There's an expectation he'll marry someone suitable to his rank."

Lucy sighed again. "Well, there's no getting around the unfortunate fact that Hawk is a duke. However, I'm not sure what Hawk's feelings are, and it's possible not even he knows. He probably has never allowed himself to examine them. I sometimes think he's been on autopilot since William and Father died—on a one-man mission, if you will, to put the dukedom back on sound footing."

Pia felt her lips pull up in a reluctant smile. "You're a good advocate for him."

Lucy nodded. "I'm biased, of course, since Hawk is my brother. But I'd also like to think I'm just returning a favor." She smiled. "After all, Hawk found me a wonderful wedding coordinator—one I didn't even know I needed. And now I'm trying to persuade you to forgive him for his mistakes—just a little, and even if it is for the second time."

Pia chewed her lip.

Lucy gave her another understanding look. "All I'm saying is give him a chance."

One part of her, Pia knew, desperately wanted to grasp the shred of hope that Lucy was giving her. Lucy had said nothing about Hawk offering love, marriage or forever more, of course. But then again, if Hawk cared…

As her conflicted feelings assailed her, Pia let herself contemplate a heretofore unthinkable possibility.

She knew she loved Hawk.

Could she remain his lover, knowing their relationship could lead nowhere? Could she let go of the fairy-tale ending that she'd always wanted?

* * *

"I'm considering keeping my relationship with Hawk…a-at least until he really is engaged to Michelene," Pia said.

Her statement fell into the conversational void like a wrecking ball crashing through the restaurant's ceiling. It was why she'd waited awhile to make her statement.

Shocked stillness was followed by commotion inside Contadini, where she, Tamara and Belinda were having one of their Sunday brunches—indoors this time in a nod to the December weather.

"What?"

"What?"

Belinda and Tamara spoke practically in unison as they stared at her from the other side of the table.

Tamara sighed. "Oh, Pia."

"Have you lost your mind?" Belinda followed up.

Pia knew Belinda's harsh judgment was made simply in hopes of jolting her from a bad decision. "I know it may be hard for you to understand."

"Try impossible."

"Belinda means well," Tamara said, jumping in.

"On second thought," Belinda continued, "maybe you have the right idea, Pia. You can always walk away from an affair."

Pia understood what Belinda meant. Ironically, Belinda couldn't manage to get *unmarried,* while she herself, the romantic, couldn't find a ticket for a trip down the aisle…

"I knew it," Belinda mused, resting one silk-sweater-clad arm on the table as they waited for their meal to be cleared. "I knew the minute that you said you were wavering in your negative opinion of Hawk that there was reason to worry. What has he done to you?"

He's turned me inside out. He makes me want to be with him no matter what.

"It makes me happy to be with him," she said simply.

Belinda rolled her eyes, and Tamara touched her arm as if to restrain her.

"That's how it starts," Belinda argued, her brows drawing together. "One minute you're having a good time, the next you're in bed thinking you're ready to gift him your body forever more…"

"Are we talking about Pia here?" Tamara asked as she and Pia stared at Belinda.

Belinda pressed her lips together. "Sorry, yes."

Tamara pulled a worried frown of her own and searched Pia's face. "Have you really considered what this would mean?"

Pia hesitated, and then nodded. She could tell, however, that Tamara had picked up on her short pause before answering.

Tamara sighed. "I wish I'd been able to warn you about Michelene. After you left Gantswood Hall, I questioned Sawyer about what he knew. It seems he had his suspicions but felt he'd received enough assurance on the matter." She pursed her lips and shook her head. "I just wish Sawyer had bothered to tell me!"

"It's okay, Tamara," Pia responded. "It's not your fault."

Belinda shook her head, her expression perplexed and disbelieving. "Have you thought this through, Pia? Because, you know, he's a duke with an obligation to produce a legitimate heir sooner rather than later. This would give you only a little more time with him. And he's misled you now *twice*."

Pia had followed the same train of thought a dozen times already, tormenting herself. She was hoping it would be a long while before Hawk was officially engaged. He'd asserted during their argument that he hadn't planned a proposal or bought a ring. Did she dare believe him?

She'd managed to leave Silderly Park with a shred of dignity and self-respect, but only by the barest of margins. Was she willing to throw her self-respect out the window now by going back to Hawk's bed with no strings attached after all that had happened?

"Perhaps Tamara and I aren't the ones to be talking to you about this," Belinda joked with dark humor. "We're the first wives club, after all."

"The first and only," Tamara modified.

"For you, I hope," Belinda said. "For me, I wouldn't mind if Colin found another wife." A look of pain flashed across her friend's face in contradiction of her belligerent tone. "But even if Tamara and I can't fully relate to the situation, we still know *you*. Do you really think you could do this—hold on to Hawk for now and then let him go?"

"It's fine for you and Tamara to be married to aristocrats," Pia replied. "But unlike the both of you, I wasn't born into a world of titles and money. I don't know much about—"

"Oh, Pia, that's nonsense!" Tamara broke in. "If I had a dollar for every bonhomie aristocrat who married in questionable taste, I wouldn't have needed Sawyer to bail out Pink Teddy Designs."

Despite herself, Pia smiled.

"Not that a marriage to you would be in questionable taste, of course," Tamara hastened to add.

"Of course not," Belinda joined in.

"Look at me, for example," Tamara went on as a waiter cleared their plates. "I always considered myself poor countess material."

Pia smiled uncertainly. It was true that, until a few months ago, Tamara had been a bohemian New York jewelry designer. But she was also the daughter of a British viscount. And she was now, in the space of a few short months, adapting well to straddling the line of what was expected of her as the Earl of Melton's wife and as a New York-based designer.

On top of it all, Tamara glowed with happiness from an adoring husband and a pregnancy that was starting to show.

Pia wasn't sure if, given the chance, she'd fare so well.

Not that she'd have that chance. Hawk had protested that he wasn't ready to marry Michelene yet, but he'd said nothing about having any serious interest in Pia.

She'd longed for a happy ending for herself since she was a little girl. Could she settle for less? Perhaps she was deluding herself into thinking a dead-end affair with Hawk was for the best.

Tamara reached across the table and touched her hand. "I don't want to hear more talk about not being qualified to be a duchess. You're more qualified than I am to be a countess, frankly, if qualifications even enter into it. You know how to throw brilliant parties and entertain impeccably."

Pia swallowed hard.

"And you are a pro at two of the most important aristocratic pastimes—fishing and riding," Tamara continued. "I find fishing deadly dull, and as for riding, I only ever do it occasionally."

Pia gave a tremulous smile, even as she flushed with embarrassment. She didn't dare tell Tamara and Belinda that Hawk was interested in different types of fishing and riding with her—ones that had nothing to do with fishes and horses and everything to do with a bed and a lazy afternoon or evening, or morning, for that matter.

Belinda looked at her too knowingly. "My advice is not to be Hawk's plaything, even if I do think an arrangement without a legally binding contract is easier. I know you, Pia, and this isn't you."

Pia looked down and fiddled with her napkin. The rational part of her knew Belinda was right. The other part didn't want to think about tomorrow and consequences. She just wanted Hawk.

She'd been young, naive and romantic once, but perhaps she was always destined to act emotionally as far as Hawk was concerned.

Michelene. Oh, God.

Pia swallowed and looked up.

Belinda and Tamara were looking at her with worried but expectant expressions.

Pia bit her lip and punted. "Mr. Darcy is waiting for me at home."

Belinda relaxed a little, obviously taking her comment as a reassuring sign. "Good girl. Learn who the good guys are."

If only, Pia thought, she wasn't still so tempted by a certain wicked duke that her stubborn heart kept insisting was her Prince Charming.

Fourteen

Hawk looked up from his desk, and then automatically rose. "What a surprise to see you on this side of the Atlantic, Mother."

It seemed as if everyone was destined to pay a visit to his office these days. Everyone, that was, except Pia.

Undoubtedly, his mother must have told his secretary not to bother announcing her arrival after obviously having taken her coat and handbag.

The dowager duchess gave him a fixed look. "I thought it would be nice if we had lunch."

Hawk's lips twisted. His mother had shown up unannounced—a clear sign that something important was weighing on her.

"What is this I hear about you and Lucy's wedding planner, Pia Lumley?" his mother asked, not disappointing by going straight to the point. "Some dreadful woman has been writing—"

"Mrs. Hollings."

His mother stopped abruptly. "Pardon?"

"The Pink Pages of Mrs. Jane Hollings. It's a column that appears in the Earl of Melton's newspapers. Specifically, *The New York Intelligencer.*"

"I don't know why Melton hasn't put a stop to it then," the dowager duchess huffed. "He's a friend of yours, isn't he?"

"Sawyer believes in freedom of the press," Hawk responded dryly, coming around his desk.

"Nonsense. This terrible woman is assailing your reputation. Something must be done."

"And what, precisely, is it you suggest I do, Mother?" Hawk queried.

The dowager duchess raised her brows and gathered herself into her full hauteur. "Quite obviously, it must be made apparent to all parties that you have no interest in Ms. Lumley."

"Don't I?"

"Certainly not. This Mrs. Hollings is suggesting that you are having the near equivalent of a liaison with the household help. The Duke of Hawkshire does not dally with those in his employ like…like—"

"Have a seat, Mother," Hawk said, pulling back a chair without breaking stride. "Would you like something to drink?"

He could use something strong and therapeutic himself.

"You are being rather obstinate, James. A simple denial will do."

"And what should I deny?"

The dowager duchess shot him a peremptory look as she sat down. "That you and Ms. Lumley are—"

"—liaising?"

His mother nodded.

"Ah, but you see, I cannot do that."

His mother stilled, and then closed her eyes briefly, as if in resignation. "Goodness. It's not just the resurrected image of you as a playboy that I need to contend with. It's the reality."

"Quite right."

He deserved every condemnation, Hawk thought. He'd dallied with Pia and hurt her. Again.

His mother fixed him with a stern look. "Well, you must put a stop to this at once. My grandfather was a renowned philanderer who left a mess in his wake—"

"You mean offspring born on the wrong side of the blanket?"

The dowager duchess straightened her spine. "We do not speak of it in this family. Kindly curb your blunt speaking. It isn't charming."

Hawk felt his lips quirk. "But, Mother, you like Great-Aunt Ethel."

"Precisely, and that is why we do not refer to the family peccadilloes. However, I still would not have the past repeat itself."

He arched a brow. "Then maybe it would be best if you did not press this matter of an engagement to Michelene. Perhaps the old earl's wandering eye could be traced to an unhappy arranged marriage."

"I had no idea I was pressing anything upon you, James," the dowager duchess huffed.

His mother had a disingenuous ability to parse the truth, but Hawk let the matter go. At the moment, there was a more important discussion to be had—perhaps one that was long overdue.

"Mother," he said with forced gentleness, "Michelene may be a lingering tie to William, but William is gone."

He'd done a lot of thinking since his return from Silderly Park, and especially after Sawyer's visit. One thing he'd realized was that he had to stop any expectations with respect to Michelene for good. He didn't love her—no matter how suitable she was—and he never would.

His mother looked at him for a moment—uncharacteristically without a ready response. And then, disconcertingly, her eyes became moist.

Hawk shifted. "I know this is difficult for you."

"William considered Michelene for his wife because she was a natural choice," the dowager duchess observed finally. "He was doing what was expected of him. He knew his responsibilities."

"Precisely, and I therefore wonder how enamored William really was of Michelene," Hawk replied. "There were times when I thought William enjoyed boating and flying so much because they were the rare moments when he could feel free. In any case, William was groomed for his responsibilities as duke from birth, and I wasn't."

His mother looked pained, but then gathered and composed herself. "Very well, but what do we know about this woman Pia Lumley?" she argued. "Where is she from? She will have no understanding of our ways and what will be expected of her as the Duchess of Hawkshire."

In the way that mattered most, Pia was well-equipped to fill the role of duchess, Hawk disagreed silently. She knew how to please him.

"She's from Pennsylvania," he said aloud. "She knows how to entertain because she's a well-regarded wedding coordinator to New York society—a respectable proving ground for women who marry well, you'll agree."

In Pia's defense, he cited the things that he knew would matter to his mother.

The dowager duchess said nothing, so Hawk pressed on.

"She knows how to ride and fish as well as any woman of my acquaintance," he said. "She is sweet and intelligent, and charmingly devoid of guile or pretense. A breath of fresh air."

"Well," his mother replied finally, "with all those sterling qualities, James, why ever would she have anything to do with you?"

Hawk laughed but it was filled with a note of self-derision. "I wonder that myself."

He was in love with Pia, and he was unworthy of her.

He'd been so intent on defending Pia to his mother that he'd stumbled upon an important realization.

He loved Pia.

Suddenly everything seemed so simple and clear.

"James?"

Hawk looked at his mother. "Yes?"

"You seem lost in thought."

"Or perhaps simply lost."

His mother stood. "Well, quite clearly I've misread matters."

"Never mind, Mother. It's nothing that can't be put to rights."

He hoped.

Hawk knew there were a few things he needed to clarify with Michelene.

And then he needed to find Pia.

If it wasn't too late, and he hadn't hopelessly botched things, this time for good...

Pia had every reason to believe that Lucy's wedding would be the worst day of her life—or near to it. In all likelihood, this day would be Michelene and Hawk's appearance as a couple, if not the announcement of their engagement.

Who else would Hawk take to his sister's wedding but his future bride? It made eminent sense.

One thing was certain: he would not be escorting her, Pia. She was working, and she supposed Hawk's days playing her gofer or man Friday were over.

Hawk's mother, the dowager duchess, would no doubt be eager to segue from seeing one of her children walk down the aisle to seeing the other married—especially when the *other* was the current Duke of Hawkshire.

But as the day progressed, it became clear that Michelene wouldn't materialize—Hawk had come alone to the wedding.

Still, Pia refused to read too much into that, and distracted herself with work.

Thankfully, Hawk didn't approach her. She wasn't sure what she would do if he did.

Instead, he remained busy at the reception, speaking with various guests and exchanging pleasantries with others.

Pia couldn't help wondering if he'd relegated her to being simply the hired help and no more these days. The thought hurt.

Nevertheless, she hungrily absorbed all her glimpses of him, storing them away for a time when she'd no longer see him.

He looked so handsome and attractive tonight that she ached.

Still, by the end of the evening, Pia was weary enough to want the night to end—if only so she wouldn't have to maintain appearances in front of Hawk and everyone else.

She had just walked out of the loftlike reception room when she heard her name called out behind her.

"Pia."

She turned around, but she already knew who it was.

Hawk.

He walked toward her, still looking impeccable in a navy suit and silver-gray tie as the evening was drawing to a close.

She looked at the clock. It was nearing midnight on New Year's Eve.

Too bad this Cinderella couldn't disappear quite yet. She'd worn a simple light blue strapless dress and matching heels.

But she didn't have a carriage, or even a car. And the wedding was slated to continue until one.

Still, she didn't think she could speak to Hawk right now.

She had to get away…get some air. *Anything.*

"I—I was just—"

He quirked a brow. "Leaving?"

Damn him. How dare he look so composed when he was the reason she was upset?

"I was taking a moment to compose myself," she replied with halfhearted honesty. "I was going to touch up my makeup."

Where was a ladies' room when one was needed? It was the only place where she knew Hawk *wouldn't* be following her.

"Why?" He surveyed her. "You look perfect."

Except for the fact that her heart was a wreck.

She sighed. "That's what women do, Hawk. They freshen up. Powder their nose…touch up their lipstick…"

"Why? Expecting someone to kiss you?"

She stared at him mutely. How could he be so heartless?

"Why disappear now?" he persisted. "It's almost midnight."

That was the point. She didn't want everyone to witness that she had no one to kiss—not even a frog. Okay, she had some excuse in that she was on the job, but still… With Hawk in the room—who knew the truth of her circumstances—that helped little.

"Isn't it customary for people to don boas and crowns and blow noisemakers? Why fix your hair when it'll get messed up anyway?" He moved a little, and Pia belatedly noticed that he was holding a small bag. "In fact, I brought some items for you."

"It was considerate of you to think of me," she said, wondering why they were having this inane conversation.

She had no plans to blow a horn or kiss anybody.

Hawk gave a little smile. "I thought it was considerate, too."

Pia thought it was too bad there wasn't another platter of hors d'oeuvres nearby.

How much would it cost her to precipitate another incident at a wedding?

Too much. She couldn't afford it.

Hawk reached into the bag he was holding and pulled out a jeweled headpiece.

It took Pia a moment to realize the tiara wasn't one of those plastic jewel concoctions that everyone wore on New Year's Eve, but the real thing.

Her brain slowed, her mind caught in a moment of disbelief.

The diamond tiara in Hawk's hand had a swirl pattern and was of equal thickness all around. Large diamonds also dangled within the swirls.

Hawk's smile was tender and thoughtful.

Her eyes, wide with shock, remained fastened on his as he moved to settle the tiara on her upswept hair.

It was the first time in Pia's life she'd ever worn a real tiara—though she'd donned plenty of make-believe ones, especially in her dreams.

"There," he murmured, easing back, his eyes meeting hers. "I have pins to anchor it in place. I've been told it's wise to do so, though I have no idea how to go about it."

Pia swallowed hard.

"I wasn't sure what color you'd be wearing," Hawk said, his voice low and deep. "So I decided to go with a sure bet. The Carsdale Diamond tiara."

She sucked in a breath, her brain refusing to function. "G-good choice."

Just inside the reception room, the guests continued their dancing and merriment, waiting for the countdown to the new year and heedless of the two people standing just outside one of the exits.

"It's the traditional tiara worn by Carsdale brides," Hawk said, his voice laden with meaning. "It was worn by my mother on her wedding day."

Pia felt her heart constrict. It pounded loudly.

She couldn't bear it if Hawk was toying with her. If this was a gambit to win her back into his bed even as he planned to marry Michelene or search for a properly-pedigreed duchess...

She bit her lip. "Why are you giving it to me to wear?"

"Why do you think?" he asked thickly, searching her face. "It's a new year and a new beginning...I hope."

"I—I don't need a tiara to ring in the n-new year."

Hawk touched her chin and rubbed his thumb over her lips.

"I know," he responded tenderly. "The question is do you need a duke who is very much in love? He comes with a big house that needs someone who can preside over large and boring parties."

Pia's eyes welled.

Hawk cleared his throat. "You once fell for plain Mr. James Fielding, and it was the greatest gift that anyone ever gave me."

Her shock turned into a crazy kind of hope as Hawk went down on bended knee. He fished a ring out of his pocket with one hand even as the other lifted one of hers.

Pia glanced down at Hawk and began to tremble with emotion. She reached up with her free hand to steady the tiara.

Hawk smiled up at her. "This is meant to match the tiara."

Pia could hardly breathe despite his attempt at levity.

Hawk's expression turned solemn, however. "Pia Lumley,

I love you with all my heart. Will you do me the very great honor of marrying me and becoming my wife? Please?"

Her first proposal. *Ever.*

She'd dreamt of receiving one—from him.

And yet…and yet…

"Wh-what about Michelene?" she couldn't resist asking.

Hawk's lips twitched. "Usually a man doesn't expect a marriage proposal to be met with a question of its own."

"Usually the woman concerned hasn't been expecting him to propose to someone else."

"Touché, but there isn't anyone else," he responded. "Michelene decided not to attend today after it became clear she could no longer have the expectation of becoming a Carsdale bride."

"Oh, Hawk." Pia's voice caught on a sob as she grasped the tiara and lowered it to her side. "I—I l-love you—" she watched as Hawk's face brightened "—and I want to marry you. B-but…"

"No buts." Hawk slid the ring on her finger, and then rose and, taking the tiara from her, placed it on a nearby table.

He took her in his arms and kissed her deeply, quieting her upset.

When he raised his head, Pia swallowed hard.

"I'm not fit to be a duchess."

"I disagree," he said tenderly. "Where else does the heroine of a fairy tale belong but in a palace?"

"Oh, Hawk," she said again. "I have lived a fairy tale. Not because you're proposing that I be your duchess, but because this was a test of character. After I found out about Michelene, I considered continuing an affair until you were officially engaged. But then I realized I couldn't do it. I loved you too much, and I wanted all of you."

His eyes sparked like brown and green flames. "You have all of me. My heart and soul."

"Your mother won't be pleased."

"My mother wants to see me happy," he contradicted. "She and my father had a happy marriage, unlike those of some of their ancestors."

"I'm not conventional duchess material."

He shook his head. "You are in character, if not background."

"But you're eminently responsible these days," she protested.

Hawk smiled. "Then I suppose it's time for me to follow Lucy in her rebellion. You know, as of today, my mother already has one American in-law."

"So far you've managed to shoot down every good reason I have for not getting married."

"That's because there are no good reasons." Hawk touched her cheek. "Pia, do you love me?"

She nodded. "I do."

"And I love you desperately. That's all that matters."

Their lips met, their bodies drawing together.

When they finally broke apart again, Hawk raised her hand. "This ring is one of the Carsdale family jewels. I didn't want to make a proposal empty-handed, but we can get you something you like better if you prefer."

Pia shook her head. "No, the ring's perfect."

"We got a second chance."

She smiled, though she remained misty-eyed. "I'm glad."

He grinned. "Your ringtone on my cell phone is the notes to the song 'Unforgettable.'"

"Really?" she inquired with a tremulous smile. "Then I succeeded. I never wanted you to forget me. It was one of the reasons—"

She stopped and blushed.

"Yes?"

"It's one of the reasons I went to bed with you again," she said in a rush. "I told myself that this time I'd leave you wanting more."

"You were unforgettable the first time."

"And yet you left."

He nodded. "Much to my regret."

"Because your brother died unexpectedly, and you needed to rush home."

"I left not because our night together meant too little," he said with a note of self-deprecation, "but because it meant too much."

"Why didn't you tell me you were Lord James Carsdale?"

"Because I'd grown used to moving around as James Fielding. It was liberating not to have to shake off women who were overly impressed by a title and money. And frankly, it was freeing for me to avoid some of the trappings of my life as a duke's younger son. Little did I know—"

"That one day you'd be the duke yourself?"

He nodded. "And that someone—someone I've come to care about very much—would be hurt by my charade."

"Oh, Hawk, we've lost so much time. I wanted to hate you—"

"But instead, deep down inside, you waited for me, didn't you, Pia?" he murmured, his voice low and intimate.

She nodded, caught by the sudden heat in his eyes.

"And I'll thank heaven every day for that," Hawk said as he lowered his head to hers again.

Pia opened her mouth under his, wanting more of him, wanting to feel their customary flare of desire.

"We can't do this here," she said eventually against his mouth between kisses. "We'll scandalize everyone."

"I hope so," he whispered back wickedly.

For he was her wicked duke.

Epilogue

"You look divine. I can't wait for the wedding night."

Pia turned from the mirror, her heart flipping over as she spotted Hawk in the doorway to the changing room.

He was dressed in a cutaway morning coat that displayed his masculine physique to perfection. She couldn't wait for the wedding night, either.

"You shouldn't be in here," she said, her words belying her feelings. "It's bad luck to see the bride…"

She'd chosen a wedding dress with an all-over lace overlay and a chapel-length train. The dress had a dreamy, fairy-talelike quality, with a straight neckline and fitted sleeves.

It was a dress fit for a princess—or a duchess.

Hawk smiled lazily. "You might feel differently about my appearance when you realize what I've come to deliver."

She surveyed him with mild suspicion. "I—I can't think what that would be," she responded, feeling the weight of the tiara that held her veil in place. "Isn't it customary to present the wedding ring during the ceremony?"

In over an hour, she and Hawk would be exchanging their vows in the chapel on Silderly Park.

"First, a kiss," Hawk said as he stopped in front of her and bent to press his lips to hers.

Pia swayed into him as she felt the warm and supple pressure of his mouth against hers.

When Hawk straightened, Pia wore a dreamy little smile. "I-if that's an indication of what you're here to deliver, then I feel compelled to warn you that we don't have the time or the appropriate easily-disposed-of attire."

Hawk chuckled, and then bent in close. "Later."

Pia felt a shiver chase down her spine at the promise in his voice. "Yes, well, first we have a major production to get through."

After the ceremony, there would be a wedding breakfast for several hundred, in a bow to the dowager duchess's wishes— and somewhat inevitable in light of Hawk's title and position. And in a few weeks' time, after a honeymoon around the Mediterranean, there would be an elegant reception in New York for those who had been unable to attend the wedding.

"After this," Hawk joked, as if reading her mind, "you'll have no end of prospective brides and hostesses seeking your event-planning services."

"I want to assure you that you'll always be at the head of the line," Pia teased back.

Hawk grinned. "How reassuring that I have first dibs on your talent as a party organizer in case I have any more friends who desire a wedding coordinator."

"I thought you exhausted all of those on your way to resurrecting Pia Lumley Wedding Productions!"

"I only called in a few favors," he disagreed modestly. "The lost veil and other capers were not my doing."

"I should hope not."

Hawk sobered a little. "This all brings me back to the reason for my sudden appearance here."

Pia arched a brow. "Yes?"

He reached over and opened a nearby dresser drawer. "I put them in here earlier," he said, withdrawing a velvet case. "I wanted to add the finishing touches to your ensemble."

"Oh, Hawk, no," Pia protested. "You've already given me enough."

"Well, that is true," Hawk conceded with a twinkle in his eyes. "The weight of my heart alone…"

She giggled.

"Nevertheless," he continued solemnly as he opened the jewelry case in his hands, "I hope you'll make an exception for heirloom earrings."

Pia gasped as she caught sight of a magnificent pair of diamond drop earrings.

"They were made for my paternal great-great-grandmother and presented to her on her wedding day," Hawk said as he gazed into her eyes. "Her marriage lasted sixty-one years."

Pia felt emotion clog her throat. "Oh, Hawk, what wonderful history and significance."

Of course, she'd replace the simple diamond studs that she wore—something borrowed from Tamara—with Hawk's gift to her.

Hawk quirked his lips. "Don't thank me just yet. My great-great-grandmother also had eight children."

"Oh!"

His smile widened as he leaned toward her. "Don't worry," he said in a low voice. "I'm already committed to raising the feline Mr. Darcy."

"Hawk?" Lucy's voice sounded from the corridor outside.

"If she finds you in here," Pia said, "she'll be sure to scold you."

Hawk stole a quick kiss. "I'll meet you at the altar."

Pia knew her heart was full to bursting. "And I'll write the fairy tale with you."

From the first day and for the rest of their lives.

* * * * *

COMING NEXT MONTH

Available April 12, 2011

#2077 A WIFE FOR A WESTMORELAND
Brenda Jackson
The Westmorelands

#2078 BOUGHT: HIS TEMPORARY FIANCÉE
Yvonne Lindsay
The Takeover

#2079 REUNITED...WITH CHILD
Katherine Garbera
Miami Nights

#2080 THE SARANTOS SECRET BABY
Olivia Gates
Billionaires and Babies

#2081 HER INNOCENCE, HIS CONQUEST
Jules Bennett

#2082 THE PRINCE'S PREGNANT BRIDE
Jennifer Lewis
Royal Rebels